T0171202

BOOKS BY ADAM PFEFFER

THE GENIUS WITH THE 225 IQ

ADAM PFEFFER

iUniverse, Inc.
Bloomington

iUniverse books may be ordered through booksellers or by contacting:

iUniverse
1663 Liberty Drive
Bloomington, IN 47403
www.iuniverse.com
1-800-Authors (1-800-288-4677)

ISBN: 978-1-4502-9711-0 (sc)
ISBN: 978-1-4502-9712-7 (ebook)

Printed in the United States of America

iUniverse rev. date: 02/17/2011

To my Uncle Stanley and David Klapper and all the geniuses in the world trying to make all the rest of us understand just what the hell is going on

"Genius only genius can explain."

WELSH PROVERB

1

The huge, bulbous head shook with confidence. On the table, the plastic tubes were lying next to each other in a large, colorful cluster.

"So you see, my dear friends, these circular tubes can be attached and strategically placed around an office or room," he was saying in that erudite, yet nasally voice of his.

They all looked at him and smiled.

"Fish will never have to stay dormant again," he explained. "Now they will be able to swim with vigorous energy."

He paused.

"I think I must doze for a moment."

The large, bulging head leaned back against one of the walls, and in a matter of minutes, Zaki Friedman was snoring.

"Utter genius," someone was saying, examining the proposed invention.

"This will revolutionize the fish business," someone else was saying.

"He really is one-of-a-kind."

Zaki didn't hear any of it. He snored away, his body at ease, until he suddenly coughed and his eyes opened. He wiped his nose with a cloth handkerchief, and then placed it back into his front pocket.

"Oh, yes, where did I terminate the explanation?" he muttered. "The fish, yes, the fish, will never have to remain in limbo—"

Zaki picked his bulging head up, and tried to focus. Most of the features of Zaki's head were bigger than most and this meant he needed more time to revive his senses. His eyes, dark brown, were large and probing, and many would say one of his long, intense stares felt as if it were going right through you. His nose was bigger than most noses, and could sniff the air with sharp accuracy. His mouth was longer and deeper than most folks, his lips red and rubbery. But it was his ears, most folks would tell you, that stood out most of all. They were bigger than most ears, and supposedly could hear things from quite a long distance away.

What made Zaki's head appear even larger than the normal head was the fact that he was only barely five-feet-tall. While his head was big and bulging, larger than most heads in this world, his body was small and shrunken, a tiny base for such a huge think tank.

Most people laughed upon seeing Zaki for the first time. They laughed and they laughed until Zaki opened his huge, rubbery mouth. Then something happened. Zaki would say something that would somehow paralyze a normal man. It was an idea, an invention, a sentence, or an opinion that was usually either fascinating or right on target, as if he alone possessed the truth and wisdom of the ages. Yes, Zaki Friedman was a genius. That was the conclusion of most people who took the time to listen to his words. Yes, a genius.

"Now you see a bowl of ordinary fish is like a bounded pond," Zaki began to explain. "There is no room for the ordinary fish to swim in an active manner. But with the 'Happy Tank,' the fish are allowed to swim from the central pond through rivers or connecting pipes. In this way, the fish can be active freestylers throughout the day and night."

Yes, a genius, a being of originality and clear exposition. In fact, if anyone bothered to ask, Zaki's intelligence quotient or IQ had been recorded as 225. Yes, that's right, the highest ever recorded in human history.

"The bounds of these connecting tubes or rivers are unlimited," Zaki was blabbing, in between snorts into his yellowing handkerchief. "They can be used to fill whole walls and entire offices."

No one bothered to challenge any of Zaki's assertions. What would be the use? I mean this guy was smarter than Leonardo da Vinci and Einstein. So who was anybody on this earth to challenge the little genius?

"You could, of course, pick any color you wanted," asked someone from the crowd.

Zaki smiled, and blew his nose. A softball suggestion. Yes, he loved when he got one of those easy ones.

"Of course," he smiled, "unless you wished for it to rotate in a multi-color pattern."

Of course. No one doubted the thing would sell. Oh, it would sell all right. Through the roof, Zaki, through the roof. Even the advance orders were astonishing.

"You could change the color of the water with the right lighting and effects," Zaki was saying, gently nudging his thick, oval glasses up the bridge of his nose. "But the main thing is that all the creatures would be swimming, yes, swimming like they would do in the wild."

Zaki blew his nose once again, and tried to smile. His nose crinkled and his lips bent upwards. He was wearing, as usual, a white shirt and black pants.

"Water is soothing," he told the crowd. "And it is the source of life and the foundation of civilization. Rivers and lakes were like the apple; they brought about a great awakening of civilization, my friends. Cities and towns and human history grew up around water, whether it be rivers, lakes, or the ocean. The Garden of Eden was most probably located near the Tigris and Euphrates. New York City became a great urban center because it has the most intricate harbor system in the United States. Yes, water, that has been the great foundation of human history—"

The crowd applauded. No one would dare challenge this little genius dozing off once again as he explained the inspiration for his intriguing invention. No one. What would be the use? He had so much information at the tips of his fingers. Who could remember so much?

"I think it would look very nice," said a small girl, holding her mother's hand.

"Yes, do you see how much work he put into it? How much interest?"

Zaki thought he heard his own mother's voice speaking to him. It was something he remembered her saying.

"Do you see all the time and patience he put into it? The boy is very good at concentrating on something that needs to be done."

Zaki smiled.

"Let's see what you've done, Zaki."

"It's a poem of some kind."

"He's writing poetry and he's not even a year old. Well, he was talking at two months, you know. I'll read it. 'They tell me I once was a monkey, eating bananas and meat, though I don't look like a monkey, I think the thought is sweet."

"Oh, Zaki."

"And he's not even a year old."

"He's very special."

"It's because he has an interest in things—"

"Where did he hear about evolution?"

"Oh, he heard one of us talking about it. Maybe he was reading about it in one of his books. He reads books you know. Not even a year old."

"Yes, excellent work."

Zaki slowly opened his eyes. He saw the small girl holding her mother's hand and smiling at him.

Zaki tried to smile back. In the attempt to smile, he sneezed, closing his eyes once again.

The small girl giggled.

"Children," Zaki muttered, after blowing his nose. "We have all been children at least once in our lives."

The crowd applauded.

"Now about the 'Happy Tank," some guy was saying. "Will it leak at all?"

"All the fittings are water-tight," Zaki replied, snorting in derision. "We have taken the utmost precautions in constructing the pipes and tank—"

"Can I examine it?"

"Go right ahead, my dear sir. You can examine the product until you are completely satisfied."

The crowd applauded once again.

The man studied the pipes and tank with intense interest, moving his head back and forth in rhythmic wonder.

"I can't find anything wrong with it," he finally proclaimed to the crowd. "The guy's a damned genius, that's all."

As the crowd applauded, Zaki attempted another smile. The lips inched up the side of his face, and then he sneezed again.

"Now if you like the 'Happy Tank,' you'll also like my other new inventions," Zaki was saying, the handkerchief fluttering in his chubby hands. "These are the computerized knife and fork, my friends, sure to make your dining easier and vastly more enjoyable—"

The crowd applauded and the small girl giggled once again.

2

Welcome to "Pop Quiz," here are today's contestants--

--An inventor and part-time philosopher, here's Zaki Friedman

A lawyer who enjoys collecting rare art, Barton Fisk—

And our returning champion, a teacher from Illinois, Debbie Nichols (Applause)--

And now to play our game—

Debbie, our returning champion, will choose first—

The question is, "Who wrote the vampire novel, *Dracula?*"

Zaki?

Bram Stoker.

That's correct for $200—

Zaki, please choose—

The question is, "What book contains the character Atticus Finch?"

Zaki?

To Kill A Mockingbird.

That's correct for $400—

Zaki, please choose—

The question is, "What was the name of the Hunchback of Notre Dame?"

Zaki?

Quasimodo.

That's correct for $600—

Zaki, you choose—

The question is, "Who wrote *Frankenstein?*"

Zaki?

Mary Shelley.

That's correct for $800—

Zaki?

World Literature for $1,000—

The question is, What book talks about "the best of all possible worlds?"

Zaki?

"That would be *Candide*."

Correct for $1,000. We'll continue after these messages—

3

Zaki discovered betting one late winter. He was reading about the college basketball tournament which took place every mid-March and decided he was going to fill out all the tournament brackets.

He looked up the statistics of each college team playing in the tournament, and then slowly and decisively wrote down his predictions. The tournament, known as "March Madness," was famous for its upsets that took place during the three weeks of play. The winning college team was crowned after the final championship game.

"These statistics inform one well of the playing tendencies of each team," Zaki explained to his little brother, Jeremiah. Jeremiah almost felt normal compared with his older brother. To begin with, his head was almost the size of a normal head, although his nose was almost as big as his older brother's. But Jeremiah wasn't complaining. His older brother might be a genius, he mused, but he was shooting for normalcy.

"So you think you can predict the winners, Zaki?" Jeremiah asked.

"There is no absolute in anything, my young sibling," Zaki replied. "But I can calculate with some accuracy who the better team might be with some degree of success."

"There's a lot of money to be won if you can do it, bro—"

"I'm well aware of the gracious compensation connected with the tournament," Zaki replied. "I only hope you can submit our predictions in time."

"I'll get them in on time, you just make the correct predictions," Jeremiah growled. "I'm looking forward to winning this pool so you better be right, my intellectual sibling."

"I have the utmost confidence in my calculations, my young brother, you just get them to the right people."

Zaki was getting ready to sneeze again, when he leaned back and shook his huge, bulging head. "Ah, yes, confidence—"

"That which can transform the prate of thunder into the power of a lightning bolt," Zaki muttered. "Yes, confidence."

"Well, we'll see how much confidence you have after the tournament begins," laughed Jeremiah. "Everyone's going to see just what kind of genius you really are, my fine bro."

Zaki leaned forward and snorted.

"That's the problem with that particular word," he mused.

"What particular word?" asked Jeremiah.

"That word, genius," Zaki finally said.

"Well, what's wrong with it?" challenged Jeremiah. "So suddenly you're not feeling up to a little basketball tournament?"

"No, the word."

"Well, what's wrong with it, anyway?"

"It's a term of violence," Zaki muttered. "Yes, a term of violence."

"But no one's doing anything to you."

'But they are using that word," Zaki protested. "They're saying wrong or right, there are some consequences for achieving some sort of recognition for one's intellectual superiority."

"Aw, come on, nobody's doing anything to you," Jeremiah replied. "You'd rather they say you were some sort of idiot or something?"

"There's so much violence in the things people say," Zaki muttered. "And usually it leads to some sort of violent act like a war."

"Just fill out the brackets, Gandhi. Or I might just declare war on you."

Zaki tried to smile. Jeremiah always made Zaki attempt a smile.

Zaki carefully began filling out the brackets. After a few minutes, Jeremiah heard snoring.

"You falling asleep again?" he shouted.

"Dozing helps me think," Zaki replied. "It takes away all the stress of living."

"Just fill out the brackets or I'll give you some stress."

Zaki's huge, bulging head began to shake.

"You ready to finish now?" asked Jeremiah.

"I believe I am, my young bro," Zaki said.

Zaki slowly filled out the last brackets. He knew there were many people who wanted him to fail, wanted to laugh and dismiss Zaki as a fraud. There were so many jealous or hateful people who knew Zaki was smarter than they were, but didn't want to acknowledge it.

"I hope you're right, my bro," said Jeremiah, seemingly thinking the same thing. "Because people would like nothing better than to criticize you in some way or laugh at your best efforts."

"Everyone can be criticized," Zaki muttered back. "No one gets out of this place alive."

Zaki handed the final sheet to Jeremiah. He was almost a foot shorter than his younger brother. Yes, Jeremiah was aiming for normalcy in every way. Zaki knew he had no hope of accomplishing that seemingly simple feat.

"I'll get it in and then we sit back and pray that you haven't lost your touch, my big intelligent bro."

Zaki snorted into his multi-colored handkerchief.

Weeks later, no one doubted Zaki ever again. The amazing genius with the 225 IQ had predicted every single game correctly on the bracket sheet. A perfect 100 percent. No one thought it was possible. No one thought even God could predict every single game. Jeremiah collected the thousands of dollars and then brought it back in a small sack to Zaki. Zaki seemed surprised as everyone else.

"The statistics were quite accurate," he simply said when Jeremiah informed him of his perfect performance. "I must admit one or two of the games did have me somewhat perplexed."

"Perplexed nothing, you were right on target. A goddamned bull's eye every time."

"Well, taking into consideration the tendencies of each team and their propensity to score in certain situations—"

"Propensity to score? You nailed every game, Zaki. Why it's almost impossible, and that's only because you actually did it, otherwise it would be utterly impossible."

"I am extremely pleased."

"Don't you want to see all the money we've won?"

"Ah, yes, the struggle between materialism and spirituality," Zaki muttered. "The quest to mix both in satisfying quanities is the key to living a pleasant life of some kind."

"It's thousands of dollars."

"I could use some of it to fund my inventions," Zaki snorted.

"Sure, sure, your inventions, my genius bro," Jeremiah said with a smile. "But right now I think we have some business at the track."

"Track?"

"Yeah, you know where the ponies run all day?"

"Would you be referring to horse racing?"

"You got it."

Jeremiah drove Zaki to the track. Zaki sneezed, blew his nose, and dozed off during the long trip. Jeremiah didn't care what the little genius did as long as he was alert once they reached the track. When the track finally came into sight, Jeremiah poked Zaki in the side, and he snorted and opened his eyes.

"This is the race track, Zaki, my bro," Jeremiah announced. "Are you ready to take on the ponies?"

"Very interesting, my young brother," Zaki replied. "I stayed up most of the night reviewing the various jockeys and horses that will be running today. It will be most enlightening to see how the horses and riders match up with their statistics."

"I always thought you get a good idea by looking at the various horses, Zaki."

"I trust in the statistics, my young bro. It is usually most reliable to know the past performances of each horse as well as who was riding them."

"Well, let's test your theory, Zaki. The first race is about to start. Who are you taking?"

"I believe Flame is the horse to choose. I like the jockey and feel the horse is due for a victory today."

"The horse is listed at 10 to 1 odds, Zaki. Are you pretty confident of the choice?"

"That would be the horse I favor in the initial race, my young bro."

That was enough for Jeremiah. If his brother was insistent of a choice, then that was the choice he would go with. He quickly put down $200 on Zaki's choice and then hoped for the best. Flame to win. He would have put down more, but first he wanted to see if Zaki knew what he was talking about. It wasn't like he really doubted his older brother, it was just he wanted to see for himself if Zaki had really done all the research he was babbling about. After all, this was real money he was betting.

"Did you place the bet?" Zaki asked.

"Darn right, Zaki dear," Jeremiah replied.

"Let's stand near the railing for the race, Jerry," Zaki said, blowing his nose. "It will give us a unique perspective when watching the race."

Jeremiah nodded, and they slowly made their way to the railing.

"Flame is number three, Zaki."

"That is good, a fine number it is."

The bugle played and the horses were directed into the starting gate. When the last horse was loaded into the gate, the bell sounded and the small gates swung open. The horses dashed from the gates, and headed around the track.

"Number three is in front, Zaki."

"Yes, very good."

"But don't you think he'll get tired?"

"Not this horse, my young bro."

No, the horse didn't get tired, and it kept darting down the track. Jeremiah was amazed how good the horse was at 10 to 1 odds. It sped across the finish line, first in the race wire-to-wire, galloping past Zaki and Jeremiah who were still standing by the railing.

"Well, I never should have doubted you, Zaki," Jeremiah smiled. "You knew the statistics all right."

"I told you I stayed up studying both the jockeys and the horses, my young brother. I knew Flame was a good pick."

Jeremiah ran to the betting windows with the winning ticket and cashed it in for thousands. The only one who wasn't surprised was Zaki.

"I like Bazooka in the second race, my young bro," Zaki explained. "The jockey is one of the most able riders at this track."

Bazooka it was. Jeremiah wasn't going to hesitate any longer. He was now a believer in Zaki's rare abilities. He would bet thousands on Zaki's choices and, just maybe, by the end of the day, the two of them would be millionaires.

"I'll go place the bet on Bazooka, Zaki. To win."

"Yes, very good thing to do, Jeremiah."

They watched the second race from the railing once again, and once again the horses flew out of the gates and challenged for the lead.

"Number six is out in front, Zaki," said an excited Jeremiah. "This is unbelievable."

"Well, taking into consideration Newton's third law of motion and average velocity times the average mass of each of the horses—"

"Look at that horse go, Zaki. How the heck did you know about him?"

"Well, as I was telling you, taking into consideration the statistics of the jockey and horse and calculating mass and velocity and the time it takes for the horses to finish the stated course—"

"Well, however you figured it out, it's going to win us some dough, and that's not some calculation, that's real."

"I anticipated the instantaneous velocity and the speed necessary for the horse to claim victory, but it was the friction involved—"

"That's it, Zaki. Bazooka won. That's two for two. We're going to be eating like kings tonight."

Jeremiah raced off to the betting window and submitted the winning ticket. It brought back five thousand dollars. Jeremiah counted the winning money with a wide smile expanding across his face. He had no doubt that his older brother was the smartest person on the face of the earth. This was going to be so easy. And then something happened as Jeremiah stepped back outside to join Zaki at the railing: it began to rain.

"Now what the heck are we supposed to do?" howled Jeremiah. "I mean of all the ridiculous things to happen—"

"Not to worry, my young brother," muttered Zaki. "I already took the time to figure out who the best mudders will be."

"What are you talking about?"

"The best mudders are the horses who have the assumed propensity to run well in inclement weather."

"You can figure for that?"

"As I have told you, the statistics tell one everything one needs to know about the past performances of each of the horses and their jockeys."

"So you know who's going to win in the rain?"

"That is correct, my doubting young bro."

"So who do we go with in the third race?"

"I am thinking it will be Thai Stick to win."

"He's coming in at seven to one."

"Excellent odds, my young bro."

"I'll bet a few thousand on him to win and place."

"That will be a shrewd act on your part, my fine bro."

"So you're not sure that he's going to win?"

"He runs well on a sloppy track, and if it continues to rain, I think he most assuredly will claim victory—"

"Then should I bet it all on him to win?"

"Whatever you prefer, Jeremiah, my brother," sniffed Zaki. "Either way we're sure to garner some amount of money."

Jeremiah decided to bet Thai Stick to win and place. It's not that he didn't trust Zaki, he just wanted to be sure to win something in case the rain should alter the race in some way.

"The race is about to begin, Zaki,"

"Yes, and the rain is becoming more intense, Jeremiah."

"Doesn't matter to you, Zaki, right?"

"It all depends on displacement as evidenced by the kinetic energy displayed by the mass—"

"Well, there's the bell. They're off."

"The track is not as sloppy as I anticipated—"

"It's sloppy enough, Zaki."

"Our horse is number eight, Jerry, and I am confident he is about to make his move on the stated course."

"Oh, yes, he's moving, Zaki!"

"Moving quite fast as I figured in multiplying mass and velocity—"

"There he goes, Zaki!"

The horse dashed down the track, the rain pelting Zaki and Jeremiah as they watched from the railing.

"We won again!" shouted Jeremiah, as the horse sped across the finish line. "I'll collect the money and then we'll leave."

"Leave, Jeremiah?"

"I don't want to stand around in the rain, Zaki, we can always come back."

"Yes, I will be more prepared next time—"

Jeremiah smiled as Zaki was still calculating the mass and speed of the various horses, the rain falling from a leaden sky.

4

Zaki make your choice—
U.S. States for $200—
What is the state flower of Alabama?—
Zaki?
The camellia—
Correct for $200—
Zaki, please choose—
States for $400—
North Dakota's state tree is what?—
Zaki?
The American elm—
Correct for $400—
So far, Zaki is the only one who has answered a question, ladies and gentlemen—
Zaki, it's your choice—
States for $600—
What is the state bird of Tennessee?
Zaki, again—
The mockingbird—
Correct for $600—
States for $800, please—
What is the state song of Utah?
--Zaki?
I believe it is "Utah, This is the Place."
Correct for $800—
States for $1,000—
What is Alaska's state bird?

Zaki?

It is, I believe, the willow ptarmigan—

Correct for $1,000—

Zaki now has $26,000. It's been a real impressive performance so far by Zaki Friedman. We'll be back after these messages and see what happens--

5

"I have the perfect solution for polluted water," Zaki was saying. "All you have to do is use my specially designed powder and the water will become crystal clear in no time at all."

The crowd gathered around him as he tapped at his glasses and surveyed the huge group of people. These conventions were essential to becoming a known inventor and selling ideas and inventions. The crowd seemed to be mesmerized by Zaki's powder to eliminate pollution.

"All you have to do is spread the powder over the polluted water and very soon thereafter you will have clear water," he was telling the crowd. "This is a must for rivers and oceans throughout the world."

"What is it made of?" someone asked.

"It's a rather simple powder," Zaki replied, "which balances the pH of the water, pollution usually being somewhat acidic in nature."

"Will it harm the fish and sea life?" someone wanted to know.

"So far, my tests have shown that most of the fish will survive," Zaki answered. "You see, my powder is very alkaline in nature and it acts on the acidity of the pollution. It also has synthetic bacteria eaters to totally clean the water."

"Why that just may work," someone muttered. "This guy's a damned genius."

Zaki had heard it all before. He had been called a genius most of his life, and now the label did not bother him at all. He went on with his explanation of the powder that could make him a millionaire several times over.

"This is a very valuable powder," he was telling the crowd. "If used properly, it could help eliminate water pollution throughout the world."

The crowd hummed its approval.

"I think it should be tested on urban waters that are extremely polluted," Zaki continued. "I was thinking that the first test should be on the Hudson River or something near it in the New York City area. I know there are many polluted rivers in that area and my powder should work on any of them."

"The Kill van Kull is one of the most polluted waterways in the area," said a female in pink stepping forward from the crowd.

She was a little taller than Zaki with wonderful brown eyes and a pretty face that would gain approval from most of the male gender.

"Yes, I've heard about that particular waterway," Zaki replied, trying not to appear awkward in any way. "I think a demonstration would be thoroughly successful."

"You're very confident of this powder," said the female with the long brown hair. "I would like to take you there myself."

"What is your name?" Zaki asked.

"I'm Beth Miller and have some authority in the area."

"I would be willing to go at any time, Beth Miller."

"Yes, and I would like to see if this powder of yours is really everything you say it is, Zaki Friedman."

Zaki didn't know what it was but there was a kind of electricity between them. He had never remotely felt anything like that before in his entire life. He wondered if Beth Miller felt it, too.

He packed up his powders and his notebooks, still watching Beth from the corner of his eye, and questioned whether this beautiful woman could have any feelings for a being like himself.

"I work for an environmental group," she was suddenly saying. "If your powder works, we would be more than happy to either buy it or refer you to a state representative."

"Whatever you prefer," Zaki replied with a suppressed snort. "I will first prove to you that it will work."

"I hope that it does," she said. "You see I want it to work, Mr. Friedman, because that would mean clean waters for everybody. I want you to know that I'm not betting against you, I want you to be successful."

"That is much appreciated, Beth Miller. I was fearful that you may want to see me fail--"

"But why would I want you to fail, Mr. Friedman? Why would anyone want you to fail?"

"It would be just human nature, I guess," Zaki explained. "I mean there are people out there who want to see people fail, it is just a fact of life."

"Not in my world, Mr. Friedman. Not when something as important as this that could benefit the entire human race. Besides, I think you're cute."

Cute? Zaki had never heard the word used in referring to him in his entire life. Cute? This is something that not even his own mother had ever said.

"Why I thank you, Beth Miller. Yes, thank you very much. It seems you have more intelligence and taste than most of the people I have ever met."

"But what about the powder, Mr. Friedman?"

"I'll let you in on a little secret, Beth Miller. This powder can be used to cure the common cold."

"The common cold, Mr. Friedman? But that would be revolutionary—"

"Yes, revolutionary. But let me tell you that the same principle used in eliminating water pollution can also be used to cure the common cold. All it will take is some alkaline powder that I have here. A cold is acidic in nature, you understand, and by using my alkaline powder, the common cold would be cured."

"Why that's very intelligent, Mr. Friedman. Have you tested it on human beings?"

"I have tested it on myself, Beth Miller, and you can stop calling me, Mr. Friedman. My name is Zaki and I would appreciate it if you used it in referring to me."

"Yes, sure, Zaki, of course. But you must tell me more about this amazing powder you have concocted."

"Well, all the work was done in my own private laboratory," Zaki explained. "The final product was completed after several unsuccessful attempts."

"And you're sure it will cure the common cold?"

"Yes, I have tested it myself. The powder neutralizes all acidic substances, the cold being one of them."

"Why that's fantastic. We'll get you and your powder to a company that will be willing to pay you for the right to manufacture it."

"You have some connection, Beth Miller? You see I don't know anybody with any kind of influence."

"But I do, Zaki."

"Very interesting, Beth Miller."

"Oh, Zaki, you can be fabulously wealthy with your inventions. All you need is someone to manufacture them, market them, and distribute them."

"And you can help me with that?"

"Oh, yes, Zaki, I will help you to become the most famous genius in the world!"

"That is more than I was hoping for, Beth Miller."

"But it's all possible, Zaki, if you just take your inventions to the right people."

"And who are these right people?"

"Oh, they are friends of my father and they will be willing to help you, Zaki."

"And you want to help me, Beth Miller?"

"Yes, Zaki, I want to help you if you will let me."

"But why?"

"Because I like you, Zaki—"

"Like me?"

"Yes, I think you're smart and cute and I like that in a man."

"Man?"

Zaki had never heard such words in his entire life. This girl, or woman, was actually making a pass at him. Could it be? Zaki had a hard time believing it. But if it was true—

"I will come with you to New York, Beth Miller," he finally snorted. "I will show you how my inventions will help change the world."

"I'm looking forward to it, Zaki."

Then Beth Miller did something no one would expect any girl to do in respect to Zaki Friedman – she leaned over and kissed Zaki on the cheek.

Zaki turned red as a beet.

"This is something that was not expected, Beth Miller," he mumbled, touching the cheek. "I think you are the nicest person I have ever met."

"And I think you're the smartest person I have ever met," she replied.

Could it be? Zaki couldn't believe it. This woman actually liked him in some sort of way. His ears were working perfectly well. He had a notion to digest the alkaline powder and see if it wasn't some sort of head cold or something.

"Well, there are a lot of other things that I could tell you about," Zaki was saying. "There's the computerized knife and fork and—"

"You could tell me all about it on the trip to New York, Zaki. Then we'll meet with the appropriate people."

She was serious. Zaki didn't know if he was ready for real scrutiny. What if he had figured wrong or something happened? Was he prepared to face the world?

"It should be very interesting, Beth Miller. I think my inventions would help a lot of people."

"Darned right," she replied. "Not only that, but you could make a lot of money from those inventions, Zaki."

"You mean we could," he suddenly said.

She looked at him and smiled. Zaki didn't know what made him say it. He didn't know why he was feeling the way he was.

"Yes, Zaki, we could all be very rich," she agreed.

"Then maybe we should get to New York as soon as possible."

She began to laugh.

"Are you ready to take on all those know-it-alls in New York, Zaki?"

"I think I could do all right, Beth Miller."

She smiled.

"Yes, I think you could do all right, too," she said.

Then she did something else Zaki had never experienced before – she reached over and grabbed his hand. They stood there holding hands as the crowd of people walked by. Zaki turned his head and stared into Beth's eyes.

Then Zaki smiled a huge, wide smile that had never appeared on his face before. He stood there grinning until Beth led him toward the street.

6

Zaki, please choose—

The question is, "What is the official language of Guinea?"

Zaki—

That would be French—

Correct for $400

Zaki, please choose—

World Countries for $800—

The question is, "What is the capital of Chile?"

Zaki?

Santiago.

Correct for $800—

Zaki, please choose again—

The question is, "What type of government does Romania have?"

Zaki—

It is a republic.

Correct for $1200—

Zaki, your choice—

Countries for $1600—

The question is, "What claims to be the oldest state in Europe?"

Zaki—

San Marino.

Correct for $1600—

Zaki, please choose—

The question is, "How many provinces are there in Saudi Arabia?"

Zaki—

I believe there are 13.

Correct for $2000—

Zaki now has a total of $45,500 and we'll be right back after these important messages--

7

The limousine slowly made its way to Manhattan, the huge skyscrapers standing at attention in the distance. Beth and Zaki sat in the back seat as the limousine scooted over the highway. Zaki was still smiling.

"Where did you go to school, Zaki?"

"School?"

"Yes, you know, what college did you go to?"

Zaki nudged his glasses, and then coughed.

"Well, I graduated from Harvard at 15," he finally replied.

"Harvard? Very good."

Beth smiled.

"What was your major, Zaki?"

Zaki snorted.

"Physics and philosophy."

Beth smiled again.

"Very good."

"I think I must doze for a moment."

"Zaki, do you realize you have the credentials to be the greatest genius who ever lived?"

"I really must doze, Beth Miller."

"Sleep? You'll have plenty of time to do that, Zaki."

"Dozing helps me relax."

"I can help you relax, Zaki."

She placed one of her slender hands on his cheek.

"Really, Beth Miller, there are certain routines I must abide by—"

"Forget your routines, Zaki, I want to help you."

"Help me?"

"I want you to be everything for me as I will be everything for you."

This was too good to be true. Zaki had never heard words such as those coming from the mouth of an attractive woman – and the words were aimed at him.

"You know that I am Jewish," Zaki finally said.

"Yes, so what does that mean, Zaki?"

"I don't know, doesn't it mean anything to you?"

"What should it mean, Zaki?"

He could see Beth looking at him with some concern.

"You don't hate me because I'm Jewish?" he asked.

"Hate you?"

"Yes, usually people hate me in some way when they find out I'm Jewish—"

"What an absurd thought—"

"You mean you don't think I killed your God and Savior?"

Beth smiled.

"Very good, Zaki, you're getting all of the stereotypes and misguided notions of the past out of the way."

"Yes, Beth Miller, I need to know if you're being genuine."

"Sincerity, Zaki? I thought that was something lacking in your people."

"Oh, we're sincere, Beth Miller, for the right person."

"And do you think I'm the right person, Zaki?"

"Could be."

"Well, I want more than could be, Zaki."

Zaki looked at her and frowned.

"But why do you like me, Beth Miller?"

"You mean you haven't had any girl tell you how exciting it is to be with someone with your intelligence?"

Zaki slowly shook his huge, bulbous head.

"A shame, a real shame, Zaki," Beth replied.

"What do you mean?"

"I mean girls are missing out on a lot, Zaki. Why I find you more exciting than any grotesque athlete or bodybuilder. I think you have more charm than the most debonair playboy. I mean you have something Zaki that a girl couldn't find in a million ordinary men. You have a fascinating grasp on reality and information. I think it would be very easy falling in love with someone like you."

"Yes, but look at me, Beth Miller—"

"All I see is someone rich beyond anyone's conception of materialism—"

"But I am a monster—"

"No, Zaki, we're the monsters."

A tear began to fall down Zaki's cheek. He looked at Beth and frowned.

"We're all monsters, Beth Miller. That is what I fear."

"Yes, Zaki, you're probably right."

She put her arm around his small shoulders.

"It really doesn't matter what one looks like, Beth Miller, does it?"

"No, Zaki, I'm afraid not."

"Then what is the answer?"

"I thought you were the genius, Zaki."

"Yes, the answer is not pretty, Beth Miller."

"No, I guess it isn't, Zaki."

"This world is filled with monsters, regardless of whether they are pretty or not."

"Yes, Zaki, I'm afraid it's true."

"They are monsters who are selfish, greedy, rude, hateful and perverted."

"Yes, that's what I thought."

"What do you mean, Beth Miller?"

"I thought you could see clearly and I was right."

"You want me to be lucid?"

"Oh, yes, Zaki, I really think we could be happy together—"

"Together?"

"Yes, Zaki, I think I'm falling in love with you—"

"What, Beth Miller, are you quite all right?"

Beth smiled.

"I'm fine, Zaki."

Zaki frowned and shook his huge, bulbous head.

"Are you sure?"

"You don't think I could fall in love with you, Zaki?"

Zaki bowed his huge, bulbous head into his small, chubby hands.

"Is this some sort of joke, Beth Miller?"

Beth frowned.

"I wouldn't hurt you, Zaki, for anything in the world. You must believe me."

"Then why play with my emotions?"

Beth picked up Zaki's huge head in her tiny, slender hands.

"But I'm not playing with you, Zaki—"

Zaki opened his large, dark brown eyes in surprise.

"You mean you actually mean what you say, Beth Miller?"

"Yes, Zaki, I think we would make a nice couple."

"Couple?"

"You surely don't think I would let you go to another woman—"

"Another woman?"

Zaki wanted to check his ears. Was this beautiful woman actually talking to him? I mean, it was almost impossible.

"I want you to know, Beth Miller, that the women, well, the women, have not treated me as kindly as you think."

"I know, Zaki, and as I have said, it is their loss."

"Don't you want to know about my new inventions?"

"Later, Zaki, now I want to know about you—"

"But I wanted to explain to you how the computerized knife and fork will work when eating a plate of food—"

"Kiss me, Zaki."

"But you don't understand."

"But you will teach me, won't you, Zaki?"

"Yes, I will teach you."

"Kiss me."

"But I don't know how to do such a thing—"

"Then I will teach you, Zaki."

Beth pursed her lips and drew her face closer to Zaki's huge, bulbous head.

"I must doze, Beth Miller."

"No, Zaki, not this time."

"Doze."

"No, kiss me."

Zaki put his lips together, and closed his eyes. He wasn't sure what was happening or what was about to happen, he only knew Beth was saying and doing things to him he had never experienced before.   Suddenly, their lips touched.

"There now, wasn't that nice, Zaki?"

"You mean we did it, Beth Miller?"

"Yes, Zaki, we did it."

"I think it was quite enjoyable. You are a very good kisser, Beth Miller."

"That's only the beginning, Zaki."

She looked at him and noticed he was snoring.

"Zaki?"

She couldn't help laughing when she realized Zaki had fallen asleep after his very first kiss.

8

Zaki, please choose—

U.S. Presidents for $400—

The question is, "Who was the first president to be photographed while in office?"

Zaki?

James K. Polk.

Correct for $400—

Zaki—

Presidents for $800—

The question is, "Who was the first president to have a telephone in the White House?"

Zaki?

Rutherford B. Hayes.

Correct for $800—

Please choose, Zaki—

Presidents for $1200—

And the question is a Double Down—

How much do you want to risk, Zaki?

I'll bet $25,000—

Whoa—

Here's the question. "He is the only president buried in Washington, D.C.?"

Zaki?

I'll say it is Woodrow Wilson.

Yes, correct for $25,000—

Zaki, it's your choice—

Presidents for $1600—

The question is, "Who was the first president born outside the original colonies?"

Zaki?

That would be Abraham Lincoln.

Correct for $1600—

Zaki, please choose—

Presidents for $2,000—

The question is, "Who was the first president born in the 20th century?"

Zaki?

That would be John F. Kennedy.

Correct, Zaki, for $2,000—

Zaki now has $74,000 with the final question coming up after these messages—

9

"Let's bring him out, Mr. Know-it-all, the "Pop-Quiz" champion and America's genius, Zaki Friedman!"

Zaki's huge, bulbous head bobbed in the bright lights as he strolled onto a television set of chairs and tables.

"Very nice to meet you, Zaki," said the female host. "Sit right over there."

Zaki sat down and tried to smile.

"Hi, Lisa," he finally said.

"Well, Zaki, it's great to see you. People say you are the smartest person in the world—"

"My mother likes me very much."

There was laughter among the crowd of people who were attending that day's taping.

"I'm sure she does, but there are a lot of strangers who are saying it, too, Zaki—"

"They're all very nice, Lisa."

"But some of them are not just being nice, Zaki. I mean you have already won $500,000 on "Pop-Quiz," and you are still the champion."

"Would you like to ask me something, Lisa?"

"Yes, who was national college football champion in 1942?"

Zaki looked at her and frowned.

"That is quite a tough one, Lisa—"

"Your people told my people that we could ask you anything in the world, Zaki, so my staff came up with this question."

"National college football champion in 1942?"

"Yes, Zaki."

"How much time do I have?"

"We're giving you just another 30 seconds."

Zaki snorted into the bright lights and the cameras and then bowed his huge head.

"But it's really not fair," he muttered.

"Answer the question, Zaki—"

"Okay, I would say the answer is Ohio State."

Everyone paused for a moment until Lisa the host began to smile.

"Yes, that's correct, Zaki, Ohio State. It's quite amazing, ladies and gentlemen."

Zaki looked up into the camera with a wry grin.

"You thought you had me, didn't you?"

"Yes, Zaki, we did. But you showed us a thing or two."

"I know my sports," he coughed.

"We thought it might be your weakest subject, Zaki."

"I don't look like an athlete?"

There was more laughter emanating through the studio.

"No, you were probably a jock in high school, weren't you?"

"I was 11 years old."

"In high school?"

"Yes, I was 11 when I graduated."

"And you didn't play sports?"

"I was in the chess club—"

"Of course you were, Zaki."

"Well, I wanted to show you something."

"Go ahead, Zaki."

"It's a computerized knife and fork and I invented them."

"Very impressive, Zaki, how do they work?"

"Well, you see, you cut any piece of food with the knife and it will tell you how many calories the food has, what the food is made of and the recommended serving for any height and weight."

The crowd erupted into applause.

"It's perfect for someone on a diet—"

"Yes, Lisa, but you don't have to be on a diet to really need my new inventions."

"No, I suppose not, Zaki."

"No, people who want to know exactly what they are eating and people who want to know how much they've eaten and people who want to know if how much they've eaten is too much for their body type will love the computerized knife and fork."

"It really is nice, Zaki. I see there is a display on both of them on which you can clearly read the numbers."

"Yes, I developed everything myself."

"And now they're available to the public, Zaki?"

"Yes, we've found a manufacturer and they will be available throughout the world very shortly."

"What are you going to do with all the money you'll be making, Zaki?"

"I really don't know, Lisa."

"Don't you have any hobbies or desires, Zaki? Maybe you want to build a big house?"

"Beth Miller will take care of everything—"

"Beth Miller? Who is she? Is she your girlfriend?"

The crowd erupted into laughter as Zaki shifted his small body in the seat, deciding how he was going to answer the question.

"Yes, Beth Miller will take care of everything," he repeated.

"Are you going to marry Beth Miller, Zaki?"

"Yes, we might get married."

"Might, Zaki?"

"Beth Miller is my girlfriend, Lisa, and she loves me very much."

"Is that so, Zaki? So now we have the real scoop. Has she told you she loves you, Zaki?"

"Yes, she has."

The crowd applauded and Lisa the host looked surprised.

"Has she kissed you, Zaki?"

"Yes, Lisa, the two of us have become very familiar."

The crowd gasped and Lisa acted surprised again as Zaki sat there with a huge smile on his face.

"How familiar, Zaki?"

Zaki snorted into the camera.

"This is a family show, Lisa."

"Yes, it is, Zaki. Thank you. Is there going to be a wedding, Zaki?"

"I can't talk about that right now, but I did want to show you my computerized pen—"

"Very impressive, Zaki."

"You see there's a display on the pen which will tell you everything you've written and allow you the capacity to print it out if so desired. There's also a dictionary and thesaurus and a spell check."

"Very nice, Zaki, but what about the wedding—"

"This is the new generation of pens and writing equipment, Lisa. They have memories and the capacity to store numerous folders and pages."

"Yes, Zaki, a great idea. I think I'll get one as soon as they come out."

"Yes, I think a lot of people will be able to use them, Lisa."

"Well, what do you think of Zaki's inventions?"

Lisa the host looked at the crowd and someone, a middle-aged woman in a pink outfit, stood up.

"I think the boy's a genius," she exclaimed. "Ain't nobody who can think of things like that."

"Yes, I think he has a computerized brain," said someone else. "I just want to know who built him?"

There was laughter and applause and then Lisa turned to Zaki.

"You have something else to show us, Zaki?"

He nodded his huge, bulging head.

"I'd like to show everyone my 'Happy Tank.'"

"Let's bring it out—"

Several men wheeled a huge display onto the stage. It was a fish tank with pipes coming out of the sides. The pipes were long and multi-colored and made their way across another wall that was being wheeled onto the stage.

"This is 'The Happy Tank,' ladies and gentlemen," Zaki was saying. "It will allow fish to swim naturally and properly as if they were out in the wild. The connecting pipes can be arranged across walls throughout an office, giving people the opportunity to watch the fish swim normally."

"Yes, a very good idea, Zaki."

"No longer will you have to trap fish in a small circular object. Now you can allow them the freedom to swim through artificial rivers."

The crowd applauded.

"Wow, Zaki you really are creative, as well as intelligent."

"Thank you, Lisa."

"All of these inventions will be available to the public—"

"Do we have time for another question?"

"Go right ahead, Lisa, I will answer anything."

"All right, Zaki, what won the Best Picture Academy Award in 1936?"

The crowd applauded as Zaki smiled into one of the cameras.

"Well, uh, I think I know—"

"Thirty seconds, Zaki."

"The answer is 'The Great Ziegfeld,' produced by MGM."

"That's correct, Zaki. Unbelievable."

"It starred William Powell, Myrna Loy and Luise Rainer—"

"Really incredible, Zaki. Zaki Friedman, ladies and gentlemen, probably the smartest person on the planet!"

"Thank you, Lisa."

"Thank you, Zaki."

"I really enjoyed myself."

"And we had a great time with you, Zaki. Why do you know so much?"

"I read a lot. I've been reading since I was an infant."

"An infant, Zaki? Well, I believe it. Zaki Friedman, everybody! We'll be right back after these messages—"

There was thunderous applause as Zaki sheepishly grinned into one of the cameras.

10

All right, everybody, let's get ready for the Final Quiz question—

The contestants will write down their wagers and then get set to answer the final question—

Okay, the bets are in—

Here's the final question—

"In the Old Testament, he led the Jews back to Jerusalem from Babylonian exile? You have 30 seconds to write down the correct answer, beginning now—

All right, time's up—

Robert?

You wrote down, Joshua, and that's incorrect. How much did you wager? All of it? Too bad. Let's go to our next contestant—

Ellen?

You wrote down, Zachariah, and that's incorrect. How much did you bet? All of it. Let's go to our last contestant, Zaki Friedman, who had $74,000—

Zaki, what did you write down?

Nehemiah. That is correct, Zaki. How much did you bet? $60,000? Yes, unbelievable, Zaki has won $134,000, a new record for the show and he gets to come back tomorrow as our returning champion with a grand total of $835,000—

Great job, Zaki, we'll be looking forward to seeing you defend your crown tomorrow. Don't miss it, ladies and gentlemen, as Zaki Friedman returns to our show tomorrow. Is there anything that he doesn't know?

Until tomorrow, goodbye everybody!

11

"Oh, Zaki, you were wonderful."

Beth stood there, looking down into his large brown eyes, and smiled.

"There wasn't anything you didn't know."

"Yes, Beth Miller, I knew all of the answers."

"And you showed everybody some of your inventions."

"Yes, the people had a chance to see some of my ideas, Beth Miller. Do you think anyone will buy them?"

Beth kept smiling.

"Yes, Zaki, they will buy them and you'll be very rich. Will you get rid of me, Zaki, after you become very wealthy?"

Zaki snorted into his yellowing handkerchief.

"I don't want anyone but you, Beth Miller, don't you know that?"

"But you'll have thousands of women just dying to be with you, Zaki—"

Zaki stopped to nudge his thick glasses up the bridge of his nose.

"How many?"

"Thousands, Zaki."

Zaki looked at Beth, and then began snorting into his handkerchief. Beth realized he was laughing and also began to laugh.

"Thousands, Beth Miller?" he finally asked with a sneeze. "You are very funny."

"I'm being serious, Zaki. You'll see for yourself."

They were walking from the studio, Beth holding onto Zaki's arm, when a couple suddenly stopped them.

"What language is spoken in Zambia?" the man asked.

"Excuse me, sir?" Zaki said.

"The language spoken most in Zambia?" the man persisted.

"Why, I believe it is Bemba."

The man looked at the woman next to him and began shouting.

"I knew he would get it," he wailed. "I should have asked him a tougher one."

Zaki looked at the couple and didn't know whether to smile.

"Good evening," he finally said.

Beth was smiling as they walked past the couple and down the dirty sidewalk.

"There now, you see?" she said. "Everybody thinks you're the smartest person on the planet now, Zaki."

"Do they?" Zaki muttered. "But what if I get something wrong?"

"We'll just have to take that chance," Beth laughed.

They were walking away, toward the waiting limousine, when a man ran up to them panting.

"Who was the NFL Most Valuable Player in 1969?" he huffed.

Zaki looked at him and then snorted into his handkerchief.

"Are you serious?" he finally asked.

"Yes, I have a bet with someone. What's the answer?"

"Roman Gabriel of the Los Angeles Rams."

"Fantastic."

The man hugged Zaki and then ran off down the street.

"I assume he won the bet," Zaki hissed.

"What did I tell you, Zaki?"

"You mean I'm going to be getting all kinds of questions from everyone from now on, Beth Miller?"

"Yes, I think so. You see everyone thinks you know the answer to every question, Zaki. They think you're a walking encyclopedia."

"We'd better get into the limo fast," Zaki replied. "I don't want to stand here all night answering all kinds of foolish questions."

"But that is going to be your public persona, Zaki."

The door of the limousine was opened and they climbed inside.

"What do you mean, Beth Miller?"

"I mean you may have to answer all of these questions, Zaki, to satisfy all of your new fans."

"Fans?"

"That's right, Zaki, these people like you and think you have all the answers and I don't think you should disappoint them."

"But what if—"

"What if nothing, Zaki."

They would have continued talking, but Zaki's phone began to ring.

"Yes, hello?"

There was a man answering Zaki on the other end.

"Who was the first English king from the House of Plantagenet?" he suddenly asked.

"Gosh, even on my phone?"

"You heard the question—"

"Henry II. Goodbye."

"Another question, Zaki?"

"Yes, Beth Miller, it seems nowhere is safe now."

"Well, we'll be home very soon."

"Home? Where exactly is home, Beth Miller?"

"Well, you'll be living with me, Zaki."

"With you?"

Zaki didn't know what to say. He almost couldn't believe it. He was going to be living with a beautiful woman.

"Yes, Zaki, we'll be living in my Manhattan apartment. You only stayed in a hotel because the show was paying for it."

"Are you going to ask me questions, Beth Miller?"

"The questions I'm going to ask you, Zaki, you'll want to answer."

Zaki smiled and snorted into his yellowing handkerchief.

"Like what kinds of questions?" he laughed.

"You'll see, Zaki. You're going to have to wait."

"Oh, I'll wait, Beth Miller—"

Zaki couldn't help snorting once again.

"Well, you'll have to because here's where I live, Zaki."

The door of the limousine opened and Zaki followed Beth onto the sidewalk. Beth grabbed Zaki's hand and hurried to the door.

"Hello, Ms. Miller," said the doorman.

"Hello, Charlie, do you have a question for Zaki?"

"Question?"

"Yes, this is Zaki Friedman."

"And how are you enjoying yourself, sir?"

Zaki snorted.

"Oh, an easy one. Very well, Charlie."

"Very good, sir."

Zaki snorted once again and they went inside. They hurried into the elevator and Zaki sneezed.

"Well, here we are, Zaki."

"Your apartment?"

"Yes, it's my apartment and now yours, too."

Zaki smiled and followed Beth inside.

"This is the living room, Zaki, take your coat off. You want anything to eat?"

"A sandwich would suffice."

"I'll make you a sandwich, Zaki, and you get comfortable. You want to read anything special?"

"What do you mean?"

"I mean is there something you want to read to keep your brain sharp?"

"No, Beth Miller." He paused for a moment. "Where do I sleep?"

"In the bedroom, Zaki, I'll show you."

"Bedroom?"

"Yes, Zaki, we'll be sleeping in the bedroom."

"We?"

"Oh, Zaki, we're both adults and I thought—"

"You mean I'll be sleeping with you, Beth Miller?"

"Yes, Zaki, that's exactly what I'm trying to say."

Zaki snorted into his yellowing handkerchief.

"Fine with me, Beth Miller," he finally said.

Zaki thought for a moment and then a huge smile exploded across his huge, bulging face.

12

The Final Quiz question is coming up—

The contestants will write down their wagers and then will get ready to answer the question—

Now the bets are in—

Here's the final question—

"It is the 39th state and is known as the Peace Garden State?"

You have 30 seconds, contestants—

All right, time's up—

Karen?

You put down Kansas, and that's incorrect. How much did you bet? Almost everything, leaving you with a dollar.

Bob?

You wrote down Oregon. No, that's incorrect. How did you wager? $5,000, leaving you with $1,000.

Now to Zaki, our leader. He had $35,500. What did you write down, Zaki?

North Dakota. That's correct. How much did you bet, Zaki? $20,000. Zaki stays our champion with $55,500 today and now a grand total of $1,100,000. Great, Zaki. Congratulations.

We'll see Zaki on our next show. Join us tomorrow as he takes on two more contestants. Until then, goodbye everybody!

13

"Well, you won again, Zaki. Did you enjoy watching yourself?"

Zaki nodded his huge, bulbous head. "Yes, it was quite enjoyable, Beth Miller. I am still the champion."

"And now you've won over a million dollars, Zaki. Is there anything you want to buy with all that money?"

"What do you mean, Beth Miller. I thought you would recommend something to me."

"Well, we could buy a house in the suburbs, Zaki."

"I don't think I have enough, yet, Beth Miller."

"Okay, we'll wait for something bigger, Zaki. Your inventions should be selling like hotcakes very soon, anyway."

"And now I am planning to write something for you, Beth Miller, so that I can show I know how to write, too."

Beth smiled. "What's it going to be, Zaki?"

"Well, first of all, I've been thinking of something men and women can go to together and enjoy—"

"And what is that, Zaki?"

"How about a sports ballet of some kind, demonstrating the various sporting events on stage and then incorporating them in an enjoyable ballet of some sort?"

"Sounds wonderful, Zaki."

"I've been thinking about it for a while, but I never committed it to paper."

"Well, I think the women would love it and the men would enjoy themselves, too. How did you ever think of such a thing?"

"Well, I was thinking of something in which sports would appeal to women and ballet would appeal to men."

"A sports ballet. Very clever, Zaki."

"I think I'll begin writing it in the morning."

"Oh, Zaki, I don't know if you'll have time. You're scheduled for a morning interview and then a taping of 'Pop Quiz.'"

"They're going to be asking me more questions, Beth Miller?"

"Oh, you don't mind, do you, Zaki dear? I think we should be going to bed now."

Zaki sneezed. "Bed?"

"Yes, you know that soft thing in the bedroom—"

"I know what a bed is, Beth Miller."

Zaki shuffled behind Beth to the bedroom. He stopped and stared as Beth took off her top and marched off to the bathroom.

"We're going to be sleeping together, Beth Miller?" he asked.

"Yes, now I told you, Zaki, we're going to be getting to know each other very well and I don't think it's such a big thing, anyway."

Zaki snorted. "Not a big thing, Beth Miller," he said.

Zaki had a feeling down below he had never felt before in his entire life. This was going to be something Zaki only dreamed about in the past. This woman, this beautiful woman, was going to sleep with him. Yes, and you know what that meant? Zaki thought about it and smiled.

Beth Miller emerged from the bathroom wearing only a bra and panties. Zaki thought he was going to faint. He put his hand on his huge forehead and groaned.

"Take your pants off, Zaki," Beth said.

"Pants?"

"Oh, don't be so modest, Zaki—"

Zaki looked at Beth and undid his pants.

"I can sleep on the couch, Beth Miller, if you want me to."

"I want you in bed with me, Zaki."

Zaki smiled.

"Of course, none of this bothers me, Beth Miller. I'm quite used to taking my clothes off—"

"Great. After you're finished, climb into bed, Zaki."

"Bed?"

"Oh, Zaki, stop fooling around and get into bed. I bet you've done this more than I can guess."

Zaki smiled and then sneezed.

"Oh, yes, Beth Miller, I have done this many times."

He slid his pants down, and then only in his underwear and t-shirt, jumped up onto the bed.

"There, that's better now, isn't it, Zaki?"

Beth's words seemed to alarm him, and he grabbed for her. Beth ended up sliding out of the bed and onto the carpet.

"Oh, no, Beth Miller, are you all right?" Zaki gasped.

When he didn't hear an answer right away, Zaki flew off the bed and landed on Beth, who was still lying on the carpet.

"Beth Miller?" he asked.

"Yes, Zaki, I'm right here," she responded. "Now you can get off me, Zaki, and climb back into bed."

Zaki snorted.

"I was just trying to save you," he said.

"Save me from yourself, Zaki?" she replied.

"Well, yes, something like that. You sure you want to sleep with me now? I could go to sleep on the couch—"

"What's the matter, Zaki, are you afraid of me?"

"Of course not, you're just a woman, a beautiful woman—"

"Get into bed, Zaki."

Zaki climbed into bed on one side and let Beth get into bed on the other side. He tried to calm himself down as if he had been doing this for a long time.

"Oh, I wanted to show you something," Beth suddenly said.

Zaki panicked, rolled off the bed, and fell to the carpet below.

"Zaki, are you all right?" she screamed.

She got out of bed and checked to see if Zaki was all right.

"It was just a little accident, Beth Miller," he said.

Beth looked at him curled up on the carpet and laughed.

"Just a little accident, Zaki," she repeated, mocking him. "Well, get back on the bed and go to sleep, we have a big day tomorrow."

"So, then, I guess we won't be fooling around."

Beth frowned.

"No, Zaki, I don't think so tonight."

"That's what I figured."

"I don't know what you figured, Zaki, but we won't be doing it tonight."

"Doing it?"

"Yes, you know, doing whatever you figured we would be doing."

"You mean making love?"

Beth stopped and smiled.

"Yes, very good, Zaki, so you're not the typical male creep."

"No, Beth Miller, I would be very kind to you."

Beth smiled again.

"Oh, yes, Zaki, I knew you would be different."

She walked toward him and grabbed his huge, bulbous head.

"Yes, Zaki, I have real feelings for you and thought we should try to get to know each other a little better before making love."

"Making love?"

"Yes, you like making love, don't you, my little genius hero—"

Beth pushed Zaki's enormous head between her small breasts. He gasped and snorted as his head pushed against Beth's body. Then there was suddenly silence.

"Zaki?"

Silence.

"Zaki, are you all right?"

Zaki smiled.

"All right, Beth Miller," he said as if in a trance.

14

Good morning, ladies and gentlemen, here's what's happening:

Congressman Bob Forn was on the hot seat today after he was heard criticizing quiz champion and all-around genius Zaki Friedman last night. "Another damned Jew who thinks he knows everything," Forn allegedly said to the crowd after his speech last night in midtown Manhattan. "The only thing they're going to win is a place in Hell," he supposedly went on to say.

No comment from Zaki Friedman this morning, although one of his associates said he will be addressing the comments at a morning television show taping.

Forn who represents a district in upstate New York has allegedly denied that the Holocaust ever took place and believes that the Jews killed Jesus. He has subsequently been reelected several times in the upstate district.

The comments came after a scheduled speech on big government as part of a fundraiser for the 45-year-old Congressman. Forn faces a stiff challenge from Millie Barden in the upcoming elections.

Jewish representatives were quick to dismiss Forn as someone who couldn't control his anger and hatred. They stressed there is much evidence to prove there was a Holocaust and that even those who don't want to believe it have to admit something occurred in Germany during World War II.

In other news, the president is getting ready to speak to Congress today—

15

The television lights were hot and bright. One of the hosts, a Patty Blake, smiled as the camera light went on and turned toward Zaki.

"We have with us today Zaki Friedman—"

"Hello Patty, it's nice to be with you this morning."

"Hello, Zaki. I know you wanted to say something about Congressman Forn's alleged comments last night—"

"All I have to say, Patty, is Hitler was a loser. That's right, he didn't win anything he set out to win. He lost the war, he lost his empire and the Jews were not exterminated. Oh, yes, there are those who still don't believe the Jews were scheduled for extermination. Believe it or not, Hitler and Germany lost in the end. That's all I want people to understand. They were losers. They lost the war, remember that."

"And what about people who deny the Holocaust ever happened?"

"They are losers, too, Patty. The Jews are still around. Now even though I know they were rounded up and put into camps, it doesn't matter anymore. No one will ever do that to us again. I'm sure of it. Because you see there were a lot of intelligent Jews who helped develop something called the atomic bomb. And now we have it. That's right, Hitler and the KKK and the John Birch Society and every other hater of the Jews in or out of the church, we have the bomb and intend to use it if our survival as a people is ever threatened again. You can be sure of it. And in the end, we will be the ultimate winners. The Jews, who so many have hated for so long, including such distinguished writers as Shakespeare, Hemingway and Oscar Wilde, will win in the end. That's right, we will be the winners, so just get used to it."

"Very good, Zaki."

"I'll give the people a question to ponder. How many Jews were actually killed in that fantasy of a Holocaust? Well, I'll tell you the answer to that one as well. Six million. That's right, an entire generation. There were six million Jews who were killed, although no crime of any sort had been committed. It was an indiscriminate slaughter in which the good were killed with the bad with no distinction between them ever having been made. Now you may not believe this sin against a people ever took place, but then what proof is there of many things, including Jesus of Nazareth. Did he ever really live? There's really no proof of it. Everything about him was decided a few hundred years later. And they blame his death on my people. That they can believe. That we, the Jewish people, who killed their enemies usually by stoning, crucified this innocent man of the people who no one is sure really ever existed. But that people are willing to believe with no argument. That we are scurrilous murderers they can believe, but that we were victims of a crazed and violent culture they cannot. Well, believe this, people: we will never be casually and malevolently murdered again. That is, not without us murdering, too."

"Oh, Zaki, do you really believe that? That you're going to be murdering people?"

"No, I don't think it will really ever come to that, Patty, but I wanted to make a point about this whole thing about not believing in the Holocaust. It bothers me and many of my people. The same people who don't believe in the Holocaust believe in the Easter bunny and Santa Claus. But they cannot believe in the Holocaust in which real people were actually murdered by a barbaric and violent culture."

"And what do you think about Congressman Forn?"

"I'll forgive him when he's kicked out of Congress as he should be. He's just another lying politician who will say anything to please the lowest common denominator. These people only care about being reelected over and over again. They protect their silly little jobs with silly little lies and don't produce much in the end. I feel sorry for politicians like Forn. They are wicked little men who parade themselves in front of the people until they are caught in some sordid affair and have no choice but to vanish once again into the haze of history."

"Would you like to say anything else, Zaki?"

"Yes, my people are a good people, as good as any other people in this forsaken world. They have their faults and they make mistakes, but so do all the other people of the world. Why they are hated more than others, I really don't know. Maybe they believe we can kill a God and maybe they believe we did. I don't think we did after looking over the other people of the world. I think we are more peaceful and law-abiding than most other people. I think we are less cruel. Yes, my people are as good as any other people, maybe better."

"Will this whole thing distract you in the upcoming quiz, Zaki?"

"No, I will be all right, Patty. Give me a question, any question you like."

"Okay, Zaki, who was the first king of Israel?"

"That would be Saul, father of Jonathan."

"Correct, Zaki, as usual. Zaki Friedman, ladies and gentlemen—"

As the television lights dimmed, Zaki looked over at Beth and wondered if what he had said would cause problems. She looked at him and smiled.

"You said what you had to say, Zaki," Beth said after kissing him on the cheek. "The human race has hated too long, someone has to speak out."

"Then you don't think people will hate me after this," he asked. "I mean, you don't think people will take offense?"

Beth looked at him and shook her head. "No, the people will get over it, Zaki," she said. "This is the game people have to play until the hating stops. Anyway, I hear Congressman Forn is going to apologize to you."

"Really?"

Zaki couldn't believe it. He thought his life in the media was over.

"No, he'll apologize, Zaki, and then everything will go back to normal again," Beth said, holding his hand and walking with him out of the studio.

As they emerged from the studio, there were little children and tall adults standing in the sunlight waving their arms in the air.

"Zaki! Zaki! Zaki!" they were screaming.

Zaki couldn't believe it. Not only was his life in the media not over, he was now bigger than ever. Zaki put his thin arms in the air, and waved his hands.

"Who was the men's college basketball champion in 1947?" someone shouted from the crowd.

Zaki smiled.

"That would be Holy Cross," he shouted back.

The crowd went wild, screaming and applauding.

Zaki felt like a rock star or a sports hero. He noticed a small girl waving to him and he walked over to her.

"Who was the Secretary of the Treasury in 1845?" she asked in a sweet, high voice.

Zaki was stunned.

"Let me think about that for a moment," he said. "I think the answer is Robert Walker—"

"Yep, he's a genius," the little girl said.

The crowd applauded again.

"Will you sign this, Mr. Friedman?" asked the little girl.

"Why sure," he replied with a huge smile across his bulbous, bulging head.

Zaki signed about a dozen signatures before he began following Beth to the waiting limousine.

"Who was horse of the year in 1944?"

Zaki heard the question and almost stumbled. He thought for a moment, remembered something, and then began to grin.

"Twilight Tear," he finally said.

"Amazing," someone shouted.

"Einstein was retarded next to this guy," someone else said.

Through it all, Zaki kept smiling and waving. He then finally got to the limousine and dove inside.

"Are you all right, Zaki?" asked Beth.

The smile faded from Zaki's huge face. He looked at her and exhaled.

"They almost had me," he wheezed.

16

Okay, ladies and gentlemen, we're getting ready for the final question—

So far, Jenny has $5,000, William has $10,400 and Zaki Friedman has $45,750—

Zaki most certainly will be back on our next show to defend his crown—

But first, we will have our final question—

Here it is, ladies and gentlemen—

The preeminent medieval philosopher/theologian, his works include "Summa Theologica?"

You have 30 seconds, contestants—

Time's up. Now let's look at their answers.

Jenny?

She put down St. Thomas Aquinas and that's correct. How much did she bet? $4,999 for a total of $9,999.

Let's go to William. He put down St. Thomas Aquinas and how much did he bet? He bet it all for $20,800. Great.

And now we have Zaki Friedman. We thought this might be a tough one for you, Zaki. Do you know your religious figures of the past?

Let's find out—

St. Thomas Aquinas is the correct answer. What did he bet? A total of $24,750 for a grand total of $70,500 today and $1,225,000 overall.

Bravo, Zaki!

Well, we'll see if we can stump Zaki tomorrow. I wouldn't count on it. This guy's one for the record books. Come back tomorrow and find out.

This guy knows everything!

Until tomorrow, goodbye everybody!

17

"We asked Zaki 'The Brain' Friedman what were the best pants to wear—"

"Zaki never gets a question wrong."

"Zaki?"

"The answer to that is Crescent Jeans."

"That's correct once again, Zaki."

"Zaki's never wrong and Crescent Jeans are the best pants to wear in the entire world."

"Zaki knows and so should you."

Cut!

The director looked at Zaki and smiled.

"Yes, you did a fine job, Zaki," he said. "Who won best actress at the 1947 Oscars?"

Zaki brushed off his gleaming pair of Crescent pants, and sneezed.

"Loretta Young for 'The Farmer's Daughter,'" he finally said.

"Yes, Zaki knows everything," sang the director. "Hopefully, the people will believe you and your very special brain, Zaki."

"I hope so," Zaki muttered. "There's a lot of money at stake."

"You're hoping for the company, Zaki?" laughed the director. "That's a good one, and what about your reputation?"

"What is my reputation?" he wondered.

"I thought you answer the questions, Zaki, my friend," said the director.

"I'll tell you what your reputation is—"

Zaki couldn't see who was talking, the bright lights glaring in his eyes.

"Why you're bigger than Joe Montana, Zaki dear."

"Jeremiah."

"Yes, my intellectual sibling, you sure are something now."

"It was all due to Beth Miller, Jerry, she turned me into a superstar."

Jeremiah stepped into the light.

"Who is that?" asked the director.

"That, my friend, is my brother, Jeremiah."

"Brother? You know this guy?"

Jeremiah smiled. "Don't believe anything he tells you," he said.

"Jerry, I want you to meet Bob Korman, my director."

"Hi, Bob, you need another genius?"

"You a genius, too, brother?"

"Well, no, not really, but nobody has to know."

"And this is Beth Miller—"

Jeremiah looked at her and his mouth fell open.

"Lollapalooza," he said.

"Glad to meet you, Jeremiah."

Jeremiah glanced at Zaki and he smiled back.

"Yes, she's beautiful, isn't she?" he asked.

Jeremiah nodded his head.

"So what's she doing with me?" Zaki asked.

Jeremiah nodded again.

"You'll have to ask Beth Miller," Zaki finally said. "Because I still don't know the reason."

Everyone laughed.

"Isn't he charming?" Beth said. "I mean how can you resist such a person?"

"He certainly is one-of-a-kind," Jeremiah replied.

"Was he always so smart?" Beth asked.

"Yes, I'm afraid so," Jeremiah answered. "I think he was reading the newspaper at nine months old."

"You're cute like your brother," Beth said.

"Cute?"

"You are brothers, aren't you?"

"Brothers? Oh, yes, at least according to Mom."

"Well, we're all going to be very rich with Zaki," she finally announced.

"He's a genius, you know," Jeremiah said.

"Yes, I think everybody knows by now."

"Except me," Zaki chimed in.

"You're always the last to know, my dear bro."

"He's very modest," Beth said. "Even in the bedroom."

"Bedroom?" Zaki repeated, not believing his ears. "Lollapalooza, and he's still around to talk about it?"

Zaki smiled. He always smiled when Jeremiah was around.

"He's actually a very sensitive man," Beth said.

"Man? Sensitive? Wow."

"Oh, don't be too surprised, Jerry," Zaki finally said.

"But I didn't know you had it in you, Zaki."

"Had what?"

"The Friedman gene that makes the ladies crazy."

Beth smiled.

"Is that what it is," she said.

"Oh, yeah, the Friedmans have been known throughout the world for having this one, sexy gene."

"Well, Zaki certainly has it," Beth agreed.

"Zaki?"

"Yes, he certainly has it."

Jeremiah turned to his brother and put his hand on his shoulder.

"Zaki, marry this girl," he finally said.

Zaki smiled.

"If you don't , I will."

Everyone laughed, and then they said goodbye to the director.

"You're going to be as hot as A-Rod, Zaki Friedman" he said, walking away smiling. "And that's no joke."

"Who said anybody was joking?" asked Jeremiah. "You're everything everyone wants, Zaki dear. Someone who can answer any question in the world and, at the same time, promote underwear. You're a natural."

"Yes, Zaki will be the real hero everyone needed," Beth said. "Someone every child could look up to and want to be, someone who earns his money by knowing everything in the world."

"Speaking of which, I came by for some lottery numbers," Jeremiah explained. "I wanted Zaki to pick them."

"But there are no calculations for such things, my young bro," Zaki said. "You might as well pick them yourself."

"No, you don't understand, my genius brother, I think even with lottery numbers you will most likely pick the winning numbers."

"But I would just be guessing, Jeremiah."

"Then go ahead, guess."

Zaki shrugged his shoulders.

"Okay, let me see, 16, 19, 39, 44 and 49."

"Yes, and the extra number?"

"26, my younger brother."

"I just won 26 million dollars," Jeremiah laughed.

"I wish it was that easy, Jerry," Zaki replied.

"Maybe he has a point," Beth said. "Maybe we should play the lottery."

"You would be fools not to," Jeremiah said with a smile. "My genius bro is pure gold all the way."

They walked to the doors, and then halted.

"Prepare yourselves," Beth announced.

"Prepare for what?" asked Jeremiah.

"Prepare for questions, my young bro, questions," Zaki replied.

"But you don't care, do you, my genius bro?"

"Not anymore, I guess," Zaki said. 'This is what the people want—"

"And so it is," Beth agreed.

Then they opened the doors, and the children came running toward them.

"Who won the Vezina Trophy in 1943?" a little boy asked.

Zaki smiled.

"Johnny Mowers of Detroit," he finally answered.

"That was too easy," said the boy standing next to him. "Who won the Gator Bowl in 1951?"

Zaki looked down at the crowd of children surrounding him and snorted. The children all giggled.

"That would be Wyoming," he finally said.

"He's a genius, there's no doubt of that," the boy said, walking away shaking his head.

Jeremiah listened to the children and began chanting something behind them.

"Zaki knows! Zaki knows!"

The whole crowd soon joined in and the chant echoed through the streets.

"Zaki knows! Zaki knows!"

Zaki, seeing that the crowd was distracted, hurried to the waiting limousine. He darted inside and sat there catching his breath.

Beth and Jeremiah soon followed.

"Zaki knows!" Jeremiah kept chanting.

Zaki smiled.

"Zaki knows when to get the hell out of there," he finally wheezed.

Beth and Jeremiah laughed as the limo sprinted from the curb into the open avenue.

18

Zaki Friedman is now the champion for the fifth straight month. He hasn't missed a question, yet. Unbelievable.

What do you have to say to the folks, Zaki?

"Thanks for watching everyone."

That's all, Zaki?

"Well, everyone knows I'm grateful for their support and hope to help many of them in the future."

Thanks, Zaki.

And now for the final question for tonight's game—

"It was the year Reader's Digest was founded?"

30 seconds, contestants—

Time's up—

Ed, what was your answer? 1927, incorrect. What did you wager? Everything. Too bad.

Julie, your answer please—

1912. No, that's incorrect. Your bet? Almost everything. You wind up with a dollar.

And now we come to our champion, Zaki Friedman. He hasn't missed one, yet, ladies and gentlemen. How about tonight?

Your answer, Zaki—

1922. It's truly amazing, but that is the correct answer. 1922. I can't believe it. How much did you risk, Zaki? $21,000 for a total tonight of $46,000 and a grand total of $1,777,000—

Unbelievable. And how did you know the correct answer, Zaki?

"I used to read Reader's Digest all the time. I once read that it began publishing the same year T.S. Eliot's 'The Waste Land' was published and that would be 1922."

Well, whatever the reason, Zaki Friedman has done it again. Can anybody stop him? We'll just have to see.

Come back tomorrow, everyone. There will be two new contestants and Zaki Friedman will be here to defend his crown. You won't want to miss it.

Until tomorrow, goodbye everybody!

19

"Who was the first Republican candidate for president in 1856?"

"Abraham Lincoln."

"Incorrect. Zaki would have known that."

"The answer was John Fremont."

"Zaki would have known that" and "Zaki would know" sizzled across the land. He had become the ultimate authority in everything. Zaki Friedman was now considered the greatest genius of all time. His picture began replacing Einstein's in encyclopedias on the internet and off when one looked up that enigmatic person called genius. He was the ultimate genius, the genius with the 225 IQ, the highest ever recorded.

"If you're such a genius, Zaki, why can't you figure how to open a little clasp on my dress?"

"I'm working on it, Beth dear."

"You can solve the hardest problem in physics and yet, you have greater difficulty opening a woman's dress. How can that be?"

"These things take time, Beth honey."

"Really now? Maybe you should invent an easier clasp to open—"

"Maybe dear. Here it is, got it."

Beth smiled.

"We could have put a man on Mars with the brain power it took to open that little clasp, Zaki."

"Very funny, Beth my dear."

Beth strolled across the room in her bra and panties. Zaki still wasn't used to seeing a beautiful woman like that, but he enjoyed every minute of it.

"You look wonderful, Beth my dear," he finally snorted.

"This coming from the smartest man in the world?"

"Yes, Beth, I do know something."

"And what is that, my genius lover?"

"I know that you're beautiful and I'm love with you."

"Is that all, genius?"

"And I want to make love to you—"

"Yes, take me, my little genius."

Zaki snorted into his yellowing handkerchief, and then got up and dashed toward Beth. When he reached her, he let her fall into his arms. Zaki's arms, however, were not meant to hold much weight, and when Beth fell backwards into his arms, Zaki dropped her to the floor.

"Muscle-bound, too, Zaki darling?" she laughed.

"Well. I just wasn't ready—"

"You can say that again."

"But I'm ready now, Beth my dear."

He jumped on top of her, and then began the screaming and shouting as Zaki and Beth rolled around on the floor. In the melee, Beth's bra came undone.

"What are you staring at, he-man?" Beth smiled.

Zaki kept staring.

"What?"

Zaki smiled.

Beth looked down at her exposed breasts and laughed. "My boobies?"

"They look like little clowns," Zaki laughed.

"Take me, darling."

Zaki reached over, and fell on top of Beth. He put his hands out to brace his fall, and suddenly realized he was holding her breasts in his hands.

"Yes, Zaki dear, they are there for you, my genius lover."

Zaki groaned, his huge, bulbous head shaking with content.

"Kiss me, darling."

Zaki kissed her, and then lying on top of her, began to moan.

"Don't get too excited, Zaki dear, we're just beginning."

Then Beth stood up and slid her panties to the floor.

"There now, we're ready to begin, Zaki dear."

"You will teach me, won't you, Beth my dear?"

"I will complete your education, my little Zaki—"

"No questions?"

"None, my little genius."

Beth then grabbed Zaki's hand and led him to the waiting bed.

20

"Are you all right, Zaki dear?"

Beth peered into the little room, wondering if Zaki had fallen asleep. Instead, she found him sitting at the table in front of the computer.

"What are you doing, honey?" she asked.

"Oh, I'm trying to solve these problems," he replied. "Nobody's been able to do it so I thought I'd give them a try."

"That's nice, dear."

Hours later, Beth returned to see Zaki still sitting at the table, scribbling on some note paper and typing at the keyboard.

"Are those problems really that important, Zaki honey?"

Zaki snorted.

"Well, they say solving each problem is worth one million dollars from this math institute in Massachusetts."

"One million dollars?"

"Yeah, for each problem, Beth dear."

"Can you solve them, Zaki honey?"

"I'm trying."

"Well, you go ahead and try your best, dear. I won't disturb you."

"Maybe you should disturb me in a few hours, dear."

Hours later, Beth returned again and found Zaki at the table, hunched over a few pieces of paper.

"How are you doing, Zaki dear?"

"I solved the first one, Beth darling."

"You solved one of the million-dollar problems?"

"Yes, but now I'm working on the second one."

"That worth a million dollars, too?"

"Yes, Beth dear."

"Well, what are we going to do with so much money, Zaki darling?"

"I think we'll move to the suburbs."

"Yes, fine, fine, that should be nice."

"And Beth, you can have anything you really want—"

"Thank you, Zaki dear."

"How about a mink coat and a diamond necklace?"

"Yes, that sure would be nice, Zaki dear."

"Just let me sit here for a while and I should be done in a few days."

"A few days?"

"Yes, Beth dear, these are some very serious problems."

"Are you coming out for meals, Zaki?"

"Yes, I'll eat, but then I'll go back to the problems, Beth dear."

"You realize you have to go back to 'Pop Quiz' next week, Zaki."

"Yes, I'll go back, Beth my dear."

"You're lucky they have a teen tournament going on this week."

"I knew that, Beth my dear, that is why I started on these problems."

When it was time for dinner, Beth returned to the little room. Zaki was still there typing at the computer.

"Zaki, are you going to eat?" she asked.

"Yes, Beth my darling, I will eat very soon."

"What about those problems, Zaki?"

"I have completed two of them."

"That's two million dollars."

"That is correct, Beth my dear."

"And how many do you have left, Zaki dear?"

"There are four left, Beth darling."

"Well, why don't you take some time to eat, Zaki."

"Yes, I will do that, Beth my dear."

After a few minutes, Zaki shuffled out of the room, his huge, bulbous head bobbing.

"I am ready to eat, Beth my dear."

"Well, let's eat in the dining room, Zaki. You can explain to me all of those problems you were working on."

"I don't know if you would really find them very interesting, Beth my dear."

"Anything you find interesting I would like to hear about, Zaki."

"I don't know if I find them interesting."

"Then why take so much time to solve them?"

"They keep my mind sharp, Beth dear. You see these problems have been around for a long time. I just thought I would solve them and help end some of the confusion."

Beth then grabbed Zaki's chubby hand and they made their way to the dining room. The aroma of the food drifted through the apartment.

"Yes, I think we'll move, Beth dear."

"If you think so, Zaki, then it's fine with me."

"Yes, I'd like to get you a nice, big house in the suburbs."

"With a picket fence, Zaki dear?"

"Yes, but I don't think I could tolerate any cats or dogs."

"So out they go."

"Yes, a nice house with a patio and a large backyard."

"You could sit and do problems all day, Zaki."

"Yes, and we could settle down and have some kids—"

"Only if Daddy agrees to help around the house."

"Yes, and I could sit and read and think about my inventions."

"And I could go to the best hairdresser in the world and the most relaxing spa around—"

"Yes, that's what we'll do with all the money."

"You mean to say you're going to win all that money?"

"Yes, about six million dollars."

"From the problems alone?"

"Yes, not to mention all that money we're making from the commercials and the quiz show and, of course, my inventions."

"Yes, we'll have plenty of loot, Zaki dear."

"Yes, we're certainly in good financial shape, Beth my love."

"Then let's get married, Zaki."

"Married?"

"Yes, let's tie the knot."

"But we don't really know each other well enough."

"Who cares, Zaki, we'll make it work."

"You want to marry me, Beth?"

"I don't want anything as much as that, Zaki dear."

"But I'm Jewish."

"So we'll get a judge to marry us."

"But my family—"

"Can't you explain to them that you've fallen in love?"

"Yes, I guess that will work."

"Of course, honey, they all want to see you happy."

"Yes, Beth dear."

"And we can get married at the Foster estate."

"A judge, Beth dear."

"Yes, a judge will marry us and we'll be happy, Zaki darling."

"Yes, I think it just might work."

"Oh, I'll make you happy, Zaki."

"Yes, and I'll have all the time in the world to do whatever I want."

"I won't let the kids disturb you, Zaki."

"Just me and you and the kids."

Zaki looked at her with a smile and then snorted into his yellowing handkerchief.

"I'd better be getting back to the problems," he finally said.

"But you barely touched your food."

"Yes, and I must doze for a moment."

"Really, Zaki, don't doze off in the middle of dinner."

"But I must relax."

"I won't bother you anymore, Zaki."

"But I want to marry you, Beth Miller."

"Really, Zaki?"

"Yes, just you and me and the kids."

"We'll have a grand time, Zaki."

"I'll explain it all to my family."

"You do that."

"I'll call my mother tonight."

"Good for you, Zaki."

"And I won't let her push me around."

"Show your backbone, Zaki."

"Who does she think she is?"

"But be gentle, Zaki dear."

Beth looked over at Zaki, but he had already dozed off. He was snoring behind his half-empty plate, still talking about that dreaded call to his mother.

"But mother, we're in love," he snored.

21

"So Zaki how did you spend your week off from 'Pop Quiz?'"

"Well, I solved all six remaining Millennium Prize Problems, Johnny."

"That's truly incredible."

"Yes, I figured them all out."

"But they were the hardest problems on earth, Zaki. How did you do it?"

"Well, one or two of them was pretty difficult, but actually they weren't that hard to figure out, Johnny."

"Harder than 'Pop Quiz,' Zaki?"

"That remains to be seen, Johnny."

"Okay, we'll see if Zaki can get through another day of 'Pop Quiz' without missing a question. Zaki, are you ready?"

"I'm ready, Johnny."

"Let's play, ladies and gentlemen."

"Zaki, you have the honor of choosing first."

"The United States for $200."

"The question is: The 50-star flag of the United States was raised for the first time on this date?"

"Zaki?"

"July 4, 1960."

"Correct for $200."

"Please choose, Zaki."

"U.S. for $400."

"Where was the 50-star flag raised for the first time?"

"Zaki?"

"Fort McHenry in Baltimore, Maryland."

"Correct for $400."

"Zaki?"

"U.S. for $600."

"The Great Seal of the United States was approved on this date?"

"Zaki?"

"June 20, 1782."

"Correct for $600."

"Zaki, please choose."

"U.S. for $800."

"What is the National Motto of the United States?"

"Zaki?"

"In God We Trust."

"Correct for $800."

"Zaki."

"U.S. for $1,000."

"Who is thought to have named the flag of the United States Old Glory?"

"Zaki?"

"I would say that was William Driver."

"Correct for $1,000. An unbelievable start once again by Zaki Friedman. He seems to know everything. We'll be back after these messages—

22

"We're speaking with Zaki Friedman, who some are calling the Ultimate Genius of the Ages—"

Zaki sat amid the bright television lights, snorting into his multi-colored handkerchief.

"Zaki, we hear you just completed the six Millennium Prize Problems. Did you find them difficult?"

"Yes, they were pretty hard, Ted."

"But you completed them in a week, Zaki. Those were some of the hardest problems in the world. How did you do it?"

"Well, I thought about them for a while—"

"That's all you did? You thought about them for a while?"

"I thought about them and figured them out."

"Well, first there was the P versus NP problem. It was generally considered the most important open question in theoretical computer science. You figured it out in about a day. Is that correct, Zaki?"

"It really wasn't that hard, Ted. I mean it included some math, biology, philosophy and cryptography, but in the end, it was pretty straightforward."

"Pretty straightforward for someone with a 225 IQ—"

"I guess that helped a little bit."

"I'm sure it did. Now what about the next Millennium Problem, the Hodge conjecture? You solved that in a day, too?"

"Yes, it wasn't that difficult, just a lot of algebra."

"The next problem was the Riemann hypothesis. What did you think of that one?"

"I finished a proof of it in a day, Ted."

"And what about the Yang-Mills existence and mass gap? That also took a day?"

"Yes, Ted, it was only a general physics problem, including electromagnetism and quantum mechanics."

"The fifth problem was the Navier-Stokes existence and smoothness. Another day for that, Zaki?"

"Yeah, that one had a lot to do with the motion of fluids. I developed a mathematical theory to deal with equations dealing with fluids."

"The last problem was the Birch and Swinnerton-Dyer conjecture. That was supposed to be a difficult one. What did you think, Zaki?"

"It was pretty hard, Ted. I struggled with inventing a new equation to prove it. It deals with defining elliptic curves over the rational numbers. One had to invent an equation to show there were a finite number of rational solutions. It was rough, but I finally completed it before I went to sleep."

"You completed all six of the problems. Were you aware that one million dollars has been offered for solving any of the problems?"

"Yes, Ted, I'm aware of the prize money."

"Then you're prepared to accept $6 million?"

"That's right, Ted, I'm going to use it to buy a nice house in the suburbs."

"A previous winner of the money who solved the Poincare conjecture has turned down the money—"

"No, I think I'll accept it, Ted. I have some things I can do with it."

"What will you do with it?"

"Well, I think I'll fund some of my inventions."

"What are these inventions, Zaki?"

"Well, the only thing we have to fear is fear itself."

"That's amazing. It sounds exactly like FDR. How did you do it, Zaki?"

"This, Ted, is the Talker, a computerized gadget I developed. You see there's a display screen with hundreds of names of famous people. You choose one of the names on the display screen and then that is the voice that will mimic any words you say into the microphone. It's a lot of fun for everyone."

"But can't such an invention be misused, Zaki?"

"It all depends on how it is used. Most inventions can be misused. It is up to the people and the society they live in to make sure such inventions are used properly. I mean I also developed a View Finder that will show you people without their clothes on. It is much like the machines at the airport, utilizing the same theory, except my invention can be folded up and placed in the pocket."

"You can get in a lot of trouble with those inventions, Zaki."

"Are they any different than a camera or a monitor? Everything can be used for enjoyment, special purposes or can be abused. The View Finder can be used by police forces and other enforcement authorities to detect theft and smuggling. It can also be abused to look at a lot of nude people. The Talker can be used for entertainment purposes or it can be used to deceive people. I mean nuclear power can be used as a bomb or to light a room. Everything can be used for the right purpose or the wrong purpose, but it should be up to the people to decide. That is the real meaning of a democracy, rule by the people."

"Yes, very interesting, Zaki. Will these inventions be available to the general public?"

"Yes, they can all be purchased at my website and will be available in various brick-and-mortar stores throughout the world."

"Any other inventions you want to tell us about?"

"I'm working on a few things right now that I don't care to reveal at the present time."

"Your inventions are impressive, Zaki, and so is the fact that it is said you can answer any question in the world. Is that correct?"

"Yes, I guess so. Do you have something you want to ask me?"

"Yes, my staff put together a few questions we thought we might ask you."

"Well, fire away, Ted."

"Okay, Zaki, name the nine Muses of Greek mythology?"

"That would be: Calliope, epic poetry; Clio, heroic poetry or history; Erato, love poetry; Euterpe, music; Melpomene, tragedy; Polyhymnia, sacred poetry and hymns; Terpsichore, choral song and dance; Thalia, comedy, and Urania, astronomy."

"Very good, Zaki, that is correct. How about if we get a little bit more difficult?"

"It's up to you, Ted."

"Okay, Zaki, what is the difference between semantics and semiotics?"

"Good question, Ted. Semantics is the study of meaning. I know that one. It involves the relationship between words. Semiotics is the study of signs and the use of signs in human communication. I think that is right."

"And so it is, Zaki. Correct."

"Thanks, Ted. I thought I had them straight in my mind."

"How about a few more, Zaki?"

"Whatever you want, Ted."

"Okay, what is a Chicago overcoat?"

"That would be a term used by the underworld for a coffin."

"Very good, Zaki, How about this one?"

"Go ahead, Ted."

"What was the name of Abraham Lincoln's dog?"

"Um, yes, that is a difficult one, Ted."

"We'll give you just a few more seconds."

"I think I once heard something about his dog."

"Ten more seconds, Zaki."

"Lincoln's dog, yes, um."

Three seconds, Zaki."

"I would say his name was Jip."

"Jip, Zaki?"

"That's right, his name was Jip."

There was silence in the studio for a moment.

"That's absolutely correct, Zaki. You got the answer with one second remaining on our clock. Outstanding."

"Well, I was just making sure if that was the name I heard associated with Lincoln's dog."

"How, Zaki, how?"

"How what?"

"How did you have even a clue on what Lincoln's dog was named?"

"Well, I read about Lincoln, quite a lot at one time and you pick up things here and there—"

"He's really unbelievable, ladies and gentlemen."

"Well, thank you, Ted."

"But we were trying to make you lose, Zaki."

"Don't I know it, but that's the game and I have no complaints."

"How about one more?"

"Fire away, Ted."

"Who was the first female general in the U.S. armed forces?"

"Well, this one I think I know."

"We'll give you fifteen seconds, Zaki."

"Her first name was Elizabeth, I know that."

"The full name , Zaki, with five seconds to go."

"Elizabeth Hoisington."

"Yes, I can't believe it but Zaki is correct."

There was applause in the studio as Zaki began to smile.

"But it's impossible, how can this guy actually know everything?"

"I try my best, Ted."

"Try? Many people try, Zaki, but you succeed."

"Thanks, Ted."

"Zaki Friedman, ladies and gentlemen. If he isn't the smartest man or woman who ever lived, I don't know anything about anything. And, folks, I know a thing or two, trust me."

"Any more questions, Ted?"

"No, Zaki, that will have to do for now. You are amazing and unbelievable and I wish you the best of luck although you really don't need luck."

"I can use a little luck, Ted, it always helps."

"Not when you have a brain like yours, Zaki. You don't need luck, you have the facts."

"The facts are sometimes not enough, Ted."

"No, I guess you're right, Zaki, as usual. Sometimes you need more than just the facts to convince people to do the right thing."

"That's right, Ted. When people are not satisfied with the facts, hit them with the truth."

"And who said that, Zaki?"

"I did."

"Zaki Friedman, ladies and gentlemen. A hero your kids can really look up to and not be disappointed. No, this kid is the real thing. Good night everyone."

23

"And now we come to Round Two of 'Pop Quiz' where the values are doubled. Louise will make our first selection—"

"Science for $400—"

"When do scientists believe the earth was formed?"

"Zaki?"

"4.6 billion years ago."

"Correct for $400."

"Zaki."

"Science for $800."

"How many types of clouds are there?"

"Zaki?"

"Ten."

"Correct for $800."

"Zaki?"

"Science for $1200."

"When was Halley's comet first spotted?"

"Zaki?"

"240 BC."

"That's correct for $1200."

"Zaki."

"Science for $1600."

"How many stars can you see on a clear night?"

"Zaki."

"I would say about 2,500."

"That's correct for $1600."

"Zaki, please choose."

"Science for $2000."

"Who discovered the speed of light?"

"Zaki."

"Armand Fizeau and Jean Foucault."

"Correct for $2000."

"We'll now go to another category. Great job, Zaki. (Applause). Yes, he deserves all the applause he gets, ladies and gentlemen. Before we go to another category, we'll pause for the contestants to catch their breath. A real outstanding job by Zaki Friedman so far and we'll go to the break with Zaki way out in front. Why don't you stick around to see if Zaki can win again? We'll be back after these messages—"

24

"This is my new invention, Beth."

She looked at the strange black object with a keyboard on top and wondered what it was supposed to do.

"What is it, Zaki?" she finally asked.

"It's a Humma."

"A Humma?"

"Yes, you see you bring the microphone attached to the keyboard up to your mouth and you hum any tune you want."

"Any tune, Zaki?"

"Anything. It can be original or a tune you've heard. Any tune at all."

"Okay."

Beth leaned over and began humming "Oh, Susannah." The small, black machine in Zaki's chubby hands immediately began playing the tune on the keyboard. It sounded very professional.

"Why that's great, Zaki."

"But that's not all, Beth."

He flipped a few switches on the machine and the song was soon accompanied by strings, horns and percussion.

"Yes, it can create a symphony out of any tune hummed or sung into its microphone."

"Why that's fantastic, Zaki."

"Yes, now anyone can write a song with any kind of tune in their head. It can produce the tune, the music sheet and even a disc."

"That's very clever."

"Yes, I was trying to figure out how to write a song without playing an instrument and I came up with this."

"Is it going to cost much, Zaki?"

"No, I think we can keep the cost down. It relies on microchips and imagination."

"Let me try again, Zaki."

Beth began singing some song she had tucked away in her brain into the Humma's microphone. In seconds, she had created a symphony of sound that twinkled through the room.

"Sounds incredible, my love."

"Oh, Zaki, this is the greatest invention of all. Why, this little black thing can turn everyone into Mozart and Beethoven. Not to mention you can have your own pop record in a few minutes."

"Yes, I think there will be a market for it."

"A market for it? Why, people will be buying them like hotcakes."

"Yes, but it doesn't end there."

"What else have you got?"

"Look at this. It's a computerized guitar. All you do is play it like a real guitar or hum or sing into its microphone and layered guitar sounds come out complete with strings, horns and percussion. You can even have 12-string guitars, banjos or mandolins."

"Fantastic, Zaki."

"There's also a computerized piano and violin. All these instruments have memories and the ability to print out the music."

"So you can write a symphony or a pop tune."

"You got it. Any kind of music you like. If you can play it, hum it or sing it, it can be produced into a symphonic delight."

"Great, Zaki."

"Listen to this, my dear."

Zaki began singing into the microphone of the Humma. In a few seconds, the tune was being played on the keyboard. It was soon turned into a melodic symphony.

"Roll over, Beethoven," he said with a smile.

"Excellent, Zaki, I think you've created some sort of masterpiece."

"No, my best work is still ahead of me."

Zaki then began kissing Beth and making sounds in the Humma's microphone. What came out was some garbled symphony.

"An homage to love," he announced with a smile.

"Oh, Zaki, now you're making a mockery."

She watched as Zaki picked up another object from the table.

"I resemble that remark," a voice said.

"It sounds just like Groucho Marx, Zaki."

"Yes, Beth, that's another thing I figured out. You can plug the Talker into the Humma and have a record sung by your favorite singing artist."

"Do you have to sing the song?" she asked.

"Yes, but I devised the machines to account for wrong notes, so they play the closest logical notes to the notes sung by the person using the machine."

"You really are a genius, Zaki. My little genius lover—"

"All you do is choose a person from the Talker's display screen and start singing the desired song."

"Choose a Beatles song, Zaki."

"Okay, I chose Paul McCartney."

"Now you start singing 'Eleanor Rigby' into the microphone and it will come out as Paul McCartney singing with a symphony."

"Excellent."

"Yes, and you can use any singer or person you want. You can have Ronald Reagan singing 'Eleanor Rigby' if you like or maybe Hillary Clinton or Oprah Winfrey."

"Wow, this is something that can amuse a whole family for hours, Zaki. We must put it up for sale right away."

"I'm sure people will be making their own records and recordings and will be selling them on the Internet in no time at all."

"Yes, you've figured out a way to make singers and songwriters independent of record companies."

"Well, that's supply and demand at work, Beth. And the royalties will go mostly to the artist involved."

"Great, Zaki, how about a Bedroom Suite?"

"My pleasure my little lotus flower."

"Hey, that was W.C. Fields, Zaki."

"Yes, do you want to hear him sing a Streisand song?"

"Very weird, Zaki, honey."

"You can't handle the truth."

"Jack Nicholson."

"Yes, how about a song from Jack?"

"How about 'On Top of Old Smokey?'"

"Yes, let's hear it, Zaki, darling."

On top of Old Smokey…

"Jack is a better singer than I thought, Zaki."

"Maybe it would sound better if Margaret Thatcher joined in."

"My pleasure, Zaki."

All covered with snow...

"I forgot all the words, Zaki."

"No problem the Humma comes with the music and lyrics to hundreds of songs that can be printed in a matter of minutes."

"Okay, Jack, take it from snow—"

"All right, Maggie, here we go—"

They sang together for a few minutes and then began to laugh.

"This really is pretty cool, Zaki. One of your best inventions."

"I was thinking of you, Beth dear."

"Let's do 'The Way We Were,' Zaki."

"As Frank Sinatra and Lady Gaga—"

"Terrific, Zaki."

They sang and laughed late into the night, until Zaki, speaking in Barack Obama's voice, finally fell asleep in Beth's arms.

25

Now we come to our Final Quiz question. The category tonight is Music. We'll find out what the question is in a moment, but first the contestants will write down their wagers to be added or deducted from their final scores—

Reviewing the scores: John has 8,500; Penny has 9,000, and Zaki has 28,500. Well, it's been another fine performance by Zaki Friedman, our champion—

The bets are all set, and so here comes the final question—

What is the term for someone who hates practicing the piano?

We'll give the contestants 30 seconds—

Time's up—

We'll start with John. What was your answer? No answer written down, I'm sorry for that. How much did you wager, John?

$8,499. You're left with one dollar—

We'll now go to Penny. Any answer? No, that's too bad. How much did you bet, Penny? Everything, leaving you with nothing and a third-place finish—

We come now to Zaki Friedman. He couldn't be caught tonight so it all depends on how much Zaki decided to risk. Did he miscalculate? I highly doubt it, but first we'll look at his answer—

Misodoctakleidist. Yes, and he spelled it correctly. Astounding and unbelievable once again, Zaki—

How much did you bet?

$19,400, for a total of $47,900, and a grand total of $3,450,000. Unbelievable. Zaki Friedman, ladies and gentlemen, is the greatest contestant of all time. He just might get to $5 million—

Well, Zaki just can't be stumped. You're invited to watch us tomorrow as two new contestants challenge Zaki Friedman on 'Pop Quiz.' Can he ever be defeated? We'll find out—

Until tomorrow, good-bye everybody!

26

It was Passover, and the Friedmans gathered in Zaki's mother's house to celebrate the holidays. Beth, who accompanied Zaki, wanted to meet the family for the first time.

"Hi, Beth, it's so nice to meet you," greeted Zaki's mother, Sarah.

"It's so nice to meet you, Mrs. Friedman, I look forward to being a part of the seder. Did I pronounce that correctly?"

"Fine, fine," replied Mrs. Friedman. "It's going to be a wonderful night."

"Name the seven liberal arts, Zaki," greeted his sister, Rachel.

"Questions, questions," muttered Zaki, shaking his bulbous head.

"Don't bother your brother," his mother chimed in.

"Oh, just answer it," his sister insisted. "Unless you don't know."

"Zaki knows everything," Beth said with a smile. "He's the smartest person in the world."

"Then what's the answer, Einstein?"

Zaki paused for a moment.

"If I remember correctly, one of them is logic," he finally said.

"Yeah, and what else?" his sister said.

"Rhetoric, arithmetic, geometry, music, astronomy, and grammar."

"What do you have to say to that, Rachel?" Beth asked.

Rachel frowned and stuck out her tongue.

"I'll get him one of these days," she said.

"Everybody says that," Beth replied.

"I have a question for you, Beth," Rachel continued.

"Yes, and what is that?"

"Why are you hanging out with my nerd of a brother?"

"Rachel."

Sarah Friedman was frowning. "You apologize to your brother and Beth," she said.

"Sorry," Rachel sneered.

Zaki watched as she hid behind his mother and stuck out her tongue again.

"She's still a little girl," he snorted.

"Bet you don't even know what to do with her," Rachel hissed back.

"Very interesting," Zaki said.

"Nerd," Rachel sneered again.

"That's like what the Hebrews had to take as slaves in Egypt," Zaki said. "I am confident Moses was called quite a few disparaging names while he was there."

"God didn't care," Jeremiah chimed in. "He spoke to him, anyway."

"And do you quite believe that, my younger brother?"

"What? That God spoke to him?"

"Yes, exactly that."

"Why not?"

"Well, do you actually believe there was some sort of being who spoke to Moses as he stood on that mountain?"

"Of course, the Torah says so."

"And you believe God wrote the Torah?"

"Of course."

Zaki tried to smile. "And what, my young bro, has this being written since that time?"

"He'll be writing your tombstone if you're not careful, Zaki."

Zaki coughed and then something like the sound of a tire deflating sizzled through his lips. "That's exceedingly wry, Jeremiah."

"It's not going to be funny when He doesn't let you into heaven—"

"And where might this place called heaven be?"

"It's certainly not near this place."

"And I suppose this place heaven is run by an old man in a gray beard?"

"How about an old woman in a gray beard, Zaki?"

"Most amusing."

"So let's see: you don't believe in God, heaven, or the Torah. Zaki, are you some kind of heretic or something?"

Zaki hissed once again. "Maybe a heathen or a pagan, my dear younger brother—"

Zaki's father, Marvin Friedman, suddenly walked into the room. "Okay, already, knock off all the *mishigas*," he growled. "We have to begin the seder."

"But Zaki doesn't believe in any of it," Jeremiah said.

"Oh, he believes," replied his father. "You know how I know he believes? Because he doubts, and doubting is very healthy when done by an intelligent member of the religion."

"So then Zaki really does believe," smiled Jeremiah.

"I believe what I must and doubt everything else," replied Zaki. "Besides my people are a fact of life and I do believe in them. Most things we believe in are myths, anyway. I mean this whole world is built upon myths."

"What are you talking about, Zaki?" asked his father. "I'd like to understand what you're talking about once in a while."

"Well, father," Zaki began. "It's like when people say Jews are this or that and don't really know anything about them. It's a myth that they cling to, and we do it for just about everything in this world. Blacks are like this, the Irish are like that. In reality, people are very different, no matter if they possess similar backgrounds. According to Immanuel Kant, the only things that matter are born with, learned, and experiential."

"I guess that's true, Zaki,"

"Yes, the whole world is based on myths. God, religion, stereotypes, all myths created by human beings and made a part of the real world."

"You're not starting with God and religion again, Zaki?"

"But they are myths, father," Zaki replied. "They're myths that have been passed down through the ages and have become a part of our society and lives without any proof or real examples of any kind."

"And who wrote the books that contain the proof of these myths?"

"The books were probably written by scribes through the ages. They're just stories, literary stories that have characters and gimmicks and provide morals of some kind."

"And all of these stories are myths, Zaki?"

"I would have to say so. There's no proof of any kind to support them."

"Well, there's proof of Adam and Eve," said his mother.

"What proof?"

"Us, Zaki, we're the proof."

"How are we proof that God created man and woman to live in a world He decided to create?"

"Oh, Zaki, you're always so confusing."

"I'm actually quite clear if you take the time to listen—"

"ZAKI!"

Everyone looked at Zaki's father, who was obviously very angry. "Don't talk to your mother like that," he finally said. "And we have to start this seder before we end up eating around midnight."

"And so we will tell the story of how the Jews were made slaves in Egypt, overthrew their oppressors, and decided to manage their own affairs in the land of milk and honey," Jeremiah said. "Now we can eat."

"You know you're getting as bad as Zaki," said his father.

"It only proves that violence has always been the one real thing that holds human history together," said Zaki, trying not to interrupt his father. "Violence and religion go hand-in-hand throughout history. There have always been wars over the gods and which ones to believe in, and there have always been violent acts committed in the name of the gods or for not believing in the favored god."

"Yeah, and what would you do, genius?" asked his sister.

"I would have some sort of Rainbow Book in which all the peoples of the world gave their version of the truth," Zaki said. "Yes, each group of people would have a chance to tell everyone what they should believe and why. You would have the Gospel according to the Italians, the Gospel according to the Irish, and so on. Each group, from the Chinese to the Japanese to the Russians to the Blacks to the Spanish to the Jews, would have a chance to have a chapter all to themselves to finally tell everybody what their version of faith and hope was. That would be the true Bible, written not by some invisible and fictional God, but by the people of the world."

"Could I write that the French were a bunch of cowardly fools?" sneered his sister.

"No, there would be no attacking, you little moron."

"Don't call your sister names, Zaki," his mother said.

"Zaki is right as usual," Beth said.

"And what do you believe in, Beth?" hissed his sister.

"Why, I was brought up a Methodist—"

"You must be very bright," his sister hissed back.

"Rachel!"

They all looked at Mr. Friedman, who was waving his haggadah in the air. "You all can believe whatever you choose," he roared. "But tonight we're going to have a seder and all of you will read the haggadah and find out why the Jews were slaves in Egypt all those centuries ago!"

There was silence for a moment.

"Slaves?" Beth suddenly gasped. "Why, that's terrible."

"Yeah, so what else is new?" Rachel said.

They all laughed, and then retrieving the wine and the matzoh, they began the Passover seder.

27

Zaki, it's your choice—
"Entertainment for $200."
The question is, "What was Captain James T. Kirk's middle name?"
Zaki?
"Tiberius."
Correct for $200.
Zaki—
"Entertainment for $400."
"Which Hollywood star played the most leading roles?"
Zaki?
"That would be John Wayne."
Yes, the Duke is correct, pilgrim.
Zaki, it's your choice once again—
"Entertainment for $600."
Oh, it's a Double Down. How about it, Zaki, how much would you like to risk on the Entertainment category?
"$5,000."
Okay, here we go—
"What is Charlie Brown's father's profession?"
You have 15 seconds, Zaki—
"Yes, um, Charlie Brown—"
8 seconds—
"Yes, I would say a barber."
Zaki says a barber—
And he's correct for $5,000—
Zaki, you choose—
"Entertainment for $800."

"How many films did Basil Rathbone play Sherlock Holmes?" Zaki?

"That would be 14."

Correct for $800.

"Let's finish the category for $1,000."

"Okay, what was the name of the Forbidden Planet in the 1956 movie of the same name?"

Zaki?

"It was Altair IV."

Correct for $1,000. Great job, Zaki. We'll find out if Zaki remains our champion after these important messages. Stick around, everybody—

28

"Welcome, everybody, to today's demonstration."

Zaki stood there in the boat with Beth standing beside him holding his special Pollution Powder canister in his chubby hands. Beth had brought them all here with her promises of witnessing an invention that would help change the world. They would see for themselves how Zaki's genius was not only being used for fame and profit, but for the benefit of the human race as well.

"I will first spread a layer of my Pollution Powder on the surface of the water," Zaki told them. "Then we will keep spreading the powder over a larger area of water until much of the water is covered. The powder contains synthetic bacteria eaters which will clean the water of its human-made pollution."

"Will any of it be cleaned up today?" someone asked from one of the other boats that were now gathered around the boat Zaki was standing in.

"Yes, some of it should be gone today," he replied. "But most of it will not dissolve right away."

Zaki then reached over the side of the boat and began spilling the Pollution Powder into the water. It was a pink powder that sparkled in the afternoon sunlight bobbing on the green water. The minute the powder hit the water there was some sort of cleansing action taking place. Soon there was a white ring surrounding the area where the powder had been spilled.

"You see, the cleaning is happening as we speak," Zaki announced to the crowd of dignitaries and media people. "Very soon, you will see that the water will become somewhat clear once more."

"What's the trick?" someone asked from one of the media boats.

"It's no trick, but a scientific process," Zaki argued. "The acidic nature of the pollution is being cleaned by the alkaline powder, while the synthetic bacteria eaters clean the pollution much the same way you would clean a particularly stubborn stain."

"Are you going to blot it all up with a huge paper towel?" someone asked.

"No need to do that," smiled Zaki. "You see the current of the water will take care of everything."

"The only problem is you need to cover a larger area, isn't that correct?" asked one of the media people.

"Yes, that's correct, which is why I brought my Boat Shoes."

"Boat Shoes?"

Zaki nodded and then produced two inflatable shoes from the bottom of the boat. They were flat-bottomed pontoon shoes with little propellers sticking out of the back of both of them. Zaki put them on his feet, and then stepped over the side of the boat.

"He's walking on water," one of the dignitaries remarked.

Zaki walked across the water in the inflatable Boat Shoes spreading his pink Pollution Powder.

"Just like Johnny Appleseed," someone said.

Everyone began laughing and applauding as Zaki slowly stepped over the bobbing green water. His shoes hardly splashed as he steadily kept moving forward.

"It's going to take him forever," one of the media people complained. "Isn't there any faster way to do it?"

It was just about then Zaki bent down and touched the metal pieces on the back of the shoes. There was a sudden whir in the water, and then Zaki jolted forward, and began skimming across the water.

"What just happened?" someone asked.

"There are motors on the back of the shoes," Beth explained. "Zaki figured out how to do one better than Jesus."

They all laughed as Zaki sped across the water, spreading his pink Pollution Powder. It looked as if he were sliding across a frozen pond in the middle of winter, his huge head staying still as it rested upon his neck and shoulders.

The media people loved it, taking pictures and video of Zaki zipping across the water, his huge ears flapping in the breeze.

"This is going to make it above the fold tomorrow," one newspaper photographer said. "Front page all the way."

Beth smiled, knowing that was exactly what they wanted. Zaki would enjoy the free publicity and his reputation as a great inventor would soar. She watched as he spread his Pollution Powder, and then came sliding back to the boat. The motors hummed as Zaki grabbed onto the side of the boat.

"Someone will have to help me turn it off," he shouted. "I'm afraid of falling into the water."

"Uh, does Mr. Christ have a problem?" asked one of the media people.

Beth smiled, and then reached down and touched the metal piece on the back of the shoes. The motors were instantly silenced.

"Whew, that was a close one," Zaki said, trying to climb his way into the boat. "I don't know what I would have done—"

Zaki's huge head suddenly fell back and he lost his grip. He fell back into the water with a huge splash.

"Some Christ," one of the media people laughed. "He better hope he doesn't dissolve and leave a white ring."

Zaki's huge head bobbed on the water, as everyone laughed. He was soon helped back into the boat by some hired helpers. He stood up in the boat, soaking wet, and put his chubby hand in the air.

"Do you see what my powder has done?" he asked.

They all looked at the water. It was somehow becoming clear in spots.

"You see?"

"It's quite amazing," one of the dignitaries said.

"You're lucky there aren't many fish," someone added.

"No, but there will be before too long," Zaki said. "There will be when the water is clear and sparkling once again like a brand new spring."

The media people gasped and kept on recording the event with their cameras and notebooks. This could be something that would save the planet.

"To celebrate the success of my Pollution Powder, I will show you another powder I have developed," Zaki announced. "It is a powder that can turn water into wine. I will demonstrate with a bottle of spring water."

"When did you catch the Christ complex?" asked someone from the media boats. "Are you going to end with a sermon about how the meek will inherit the earth?"

Zaki smiled. "No, but I did want to show you how God can be recreated in the laboratory," he said. "By pouring the wine powder in the water, I will show you how the task was performed."

"Do you have a beer for me, Mr. Christ?" a reporter asked.

Zaki smiled once again. "As a matter of fact, I do have beer powder back in my lab. I thought the wine powder would be more appreciated in keeping with the Boat Shoes and the walking on water."

"Are you trying to get us all drunk?" someone asked.

"Not really," Zaki said. "I just wanted to show you just how close we are to recreating God."

"He's not going to like that," someone laughed.

"Then let Him do something about it," Zaki replied.

"You're not doubting the existence of God, are you?"

"Maybe so, but that doesn't really matter at the present time. The only thing that matters is that the ways of God are now among us."

"Are you saying you're God?"

"No, of course not," Zaki shot back. "I'm just telling you there are ways to recreate God and then use his ways to help people."

"Do we have to bow down to you?"

"No, no, people, I'm just demonstrating how the ways of God can help us all in the years ahead."

"You're not going to start preaching, are you?"

"No, no, but look at the water."

The water was becoming clear, although someone spotted a dead fish floating on the surface.

"Uh, Mr. Christ, I think you have to bring this back to life," one of the reporters laughed.

"But I can't do that," Zaki answered.

"Some God you turned out to be."

Everyone began laughing, and then Zaki began passing around the water he had changed to wine.

"Today is a good year," one of the reporters laughed. He then began to drink the wine. "It isn't that bad," he finally said. "Maybe it will dissolve all the pollution inside of me."

Everyone passed around the wine and took a sip. "Now who is going to betray him with a kiss?" one of the reporters asked.

"You see, it tastes quite good," Zaki said.

"Are you trying to get us plastered, Mr. Christ?"

"No, I just wanted you to experience the wonders of the Lord."

"You're nice, Mr. Christ," one of the photographers chimed in.

"Thank you all for your attention," Zaki said.

"We can all go back now?" asked one of the dignitaries.

"Well, I thought you might want to stay a little longer to see if the water clears up."

"Will it happen today?"

"It could. I'm not sure anymore."

So they stood in the boats and studied the water. There were patches of clear water, but the water was still mostly green.

"Any questions?" Zaki asked.

"Yeah, who's paying for all of this?" one reporter asked.

"I am," Zaki replied.

"Good, I thought the people were going to be billed—"

"And what if they were?" Beth grumbled. "Why Zaki's powder may put an end to polluted water."

"But his wine may give rise to a polluted population," said one of the reporters.

"Anyway, his powders may also cure the common cold," Beth explained. "All you have to do is rub it on your nose and the powder will keep away the cold."

"Can you use it for a hangover?" laughed one of the reporters.

"The water's clearing up," Zaki interrupted. "You see, everybody, how the green tinge is disappearing."

"When do the dead bodies begin to rise?"

"Dead bodies?"

"Yeah, will your powder dissolve cement?"

"There will be very few dead things when I'm done," Zaki promised the crowd. "And there will be new life taking its place tomorrow."

"Okay, genius, what if it does work? Then what? Do we have to pay you to get rid of all the pollution?"

"Good question," Zaki replied. "We will gladly help out the city at a reduced cost to the taxpayers."

"Then you're going to charge everybody?"

"Well, that's only fair," Zaki insisted. "I mean I should get something for all of this, don't you agree?"

"Ah, the same old thing," one of the reporters said. "You're just doing this for the money—"

Zaki took out his yellowing handkerchief and snorted into it. "I want to help the world more than you know," he argued. "But one must think about his own family once in a while."

"Yeah, sure, you're doing it for the world," a reporter said.

"I must doze for a moment."

"Doze?"

"Yes, I need to rest for a moment."

Zaki sat down in the boat and immediately began snoring.

"Is he on drugs or something," asked one of the reporters.

"Had a late-night party?"

"Zaki just needed to rest," Beth explained. "It's been very stressful for him and this is how he copes with it."

"Is that possible?" a reporter asked. "To just sit down and fall asleep? Does he have some kind of disease or something?"

"No, it's just his way," Beth said.

"Well, wake him up," one of the dignitaries complained. "We don't want to just sit here and watch him snore."

Beth bent down and tapped Zaki on the shoulder. Nothing happened. She shook his arm and nothing happened. She finally pushed him and Zaki's eyes fluttered open.

"Yes, the water's clearing up," he was muttering. "You see how the powder is doing its job?"

Everyone laughed as Zaki kept muttering to no one in particular.

"He's been resurrected," someone said.

"Now about the powder—"

"Great job, Mr. Clean, can we go back now?"

"I suggest we return tomorrow, ladies and gentlemen."

"Yeah, right," one of the reporters said. "You'll be wrapping fish by then."

"But you see how the powder is cleansing the water?"

"Yes, you've done a great job, Zaki," Beth said.

"Yes, terrific," someone said. "Are you going to walk on it again?"

"Maybe tomorrow."

Then they all sat back down in the boats, the media people and the dignitaries, and headed back to shore. The roaring of the motors was the only noise one could hear. No one noticed Zaki snoring once again in the back of one of the boats.

29

Zaki, it's your choice in this second round of "Pop Quiz."
Religion for $400—
What does the name Islam mean?
Zaki?
Submission.
Correct for $400.
Please choose, Zaki—
Religion for $800—
Who was the first pope?
Zaki—
Peter.
Correct for $800—
It's your choice, Zaki—
Religion for $1200—
What was the first plague of Egypt?
Zaki?
The waters turned to blood.
Correct for $1200—
Zaki, it's your choice—
Religion for $1600—
What does the word, avatar, mean to a Hindu?
Zaki—
The human incarnation of a god.
Correct for $1600—
Zaki, it's your choice—
Let's finish the category, Religion for $2000—

Oh, it's a Double Down. How much are you going to risk on Religion, Zaki?

$20,000.

Oh, wow, Zaki, there's a whole lot of money on the line. I'll read the question and then you'll have 15 seconds, Zaki, to answer it. Okay? Here's the question: What were the names of the criminals crucified at the same time as Jesus?

You have 15 seconds—

This is a tough one.

Do you have an answer, Zaki?

7 seconds remaining—

Now there's six—

Five—

Well, there's really no answer.

Yes, Zaki?

Well, usually it's two thieves named Dismas and Gestas, but the Bible really doesn't say—

That's absolutely correct, Zaki. Unbelievable. That's for $20,000—

Thank you.

Just unbelievable, ladies and gentlemen. Zaki just can't be stumped. We're going to take a break, but we'll continue our game after these messages—

30

Beth peered into the little room with the computer and found Zaki huddled in front of the keyboard.

"I've almost completed the Sports Ballet," he said, noticing her staring at him. "It will be an ode to love and sports."

"Why love?" she asked.

"Because it is you, my dear, who inspired me to write it. I think it will be something couples will come to see."

"But it is about sports, right, Zaki?"

"Yes, to keep the men interested in what is going on."

"And what's going on?"

"A love story involving a man and a woman and their love of sports."

"Is there a competition between them?"

"Yes, but in the end, they discover how to team up and compete against others."

"Sounds terrific, Zaki."

"Yes, Zaki Friedman's Sports Ballet."

"You'll make a lot of men and women happy, Zaki."

"Yes, now they can be together and both enjoy a form of entertainment that incorporates two kinds of entertainment they prefer."

"But it is entertainment, when separated, would cause them to go their separate ways."

"Yes, something like that, my dear."

"So how are you going to do it?"

"Well, first there is an ode to baseball."

"Ah, the national game."

"Yes, but we go through the history of the game from the 1800s—"

"All played out in dance and ballet."

"Yes, with twirls and lifts and spins."

"All in baseball uniforms."

"Yes, and with bats and balls and gloves."

"Tremendous."

"Yes, and Babe Ruth and Lou Gehrig and Walter Johnson."

"All leading up to Jackie Robinson and the integration of the major leagues."

"Yes, like that."

"And there will be sliding and bunting—"

"Yes, my dear, and stealing and mammoth home runs."

"Oh, Zaki, you'll be able to taste the hot dogs."

"And feel the excitement of the park."

"And there will be singing."

"Oh, yes, I've written a variation of 'Take Me Out to the Ballgame' which can be played by a full orchestra."

"And what about the 'Star-Spangled Banner?"

"Yes, that, too."

"Oh, it will be a grand evening, Zaki, for everyone, the whole family."

"Yes, but that's not all."

"What do you mean?"

"Well, once we're finished with baseball, it's off to football."

"Yes, the tackling and passing."

"The hitting and running."

"All expressed through pirouettes and plies, Zaki dear."

"Of course, my love."

"The stage filled with dancers in uniforms and shoulder pads."

"There will be cheerleaders and coaches and all kinds of dancing."

"And there will be music."

"Yes, something I've written on the Humma."

"Wonderful, Zaki."

"And we will go through the different eras of football uniforms."

"And end up in the present."

"Yes, dear, it will feel like you're sitting in a stadium."

"Marvelous."

"But that's not all."

"Oh, no, darling, there are more sporting events."

"Yes, an ode to basketball."

"Very exciting."

"With baskets and backboards rolled onto the stage."

"A ball being passed among the dancers as they hurry down the court."

"Yes, and the shooting and dunking."

"The shorts and the tutus."

"Yes, my love, and the twirling and dancing."

"All the action of a real game."

"Yes, but so much more."

"Oh, Zaki, it sounds fantastic, I can hardly wait."

"You'll see it all sooner than you think."

"When does it open?"

"In a few days, but I haven't finished telling you about all the sports involved."

"I have to buy a new dress for opening night."

"Yes, I will rent a tux, but I'm not finished."

"I have to get my hair done."

"But we still haven't settled on a definite date, Beth."

"But you have to give me a few days, Zaki, to get ready."

"I don't even know what day they will decide on."

"But all the things we have to do."

"Did I tell you there was an ode to ice hockey?"

"With real skating and ice, Zaki?"

"No, we'll simulate that on the stage, but it will be very authentic nonetheless."

"There's going to be hitting and fighting, Zaki?"

"Yes, and goalies and gloves and all kinds of sliding and twirling."

"Sounds like a lot of fun, Zaki."

"Oh, it will be, I'll guarantee that."

"And what about golf and tennis and boxing and wrestling?"

"We'll have all of it, Beth dear."

"But how is there enough time, Zaki?"

"Oh, there's enough time to do most of it. I'm going to write another ballet that includes the Olympics, Summer and Winter."

"Yes, jumping and running and throwing."

"And skating and skiing and gymnastics."

"Oh, it certainly will be thrilling, Zaki."

"Yes, another ballet that man and woman and the whole family can go to and enjoy without boring anyone."

"Yes, something everyone can enjoy."

"This one will have boxing and wrestling."

"But don't make it too violent, Zaki."

"No, I know my audience will be women and children and their men."

"Yes, maybe you should include swimming and diving."

"In the Olympic ballet, my dear. This one will only be able to do the major sports that families attend."

"But you need something for women."

"Yes, I'll have some figure skating after the ice hockey."

"Yes, the women and female children will enjoy that, Zaki."

"Yes, everyone will be entertained."

"Just as it should be, Zaki."

"I'll have the women play tennis and demonstrate figure skating and be cheerleaders for the men's sports."

"Yes, have them cheer, but show them winning at their own contests, Zaki. That's the only fair thing to do."

"Yes, we will have women champions and men champions and everyone will be satisfied."

"Yes, give the people what they want, Zaki."

"And they want everyone to win at something."

"Yes, Zaki, that's it."

"Everyone winning and sharing their joy with each other as they compete in the world of sports."

"That's what you have to do, Zaki."

"Then you think it will be a hit?"

"Of course, dear."

"And everyone will be satisfied in the end?"

"That's how it looks to me, Zaki."

"We'll do the Super Bowl."

"Yes, dear."

"The World Series."

"Yes, Zaki."

"The Stanley Cup."

"Oh, yes, very good."

"The championships."

"Yes, very exciting."

"The champions of champions."

"Zaki, you'd better calm down."

He sneezed and then snorted into his yellowing handkerchief.

"Are you all right, Zaki?"

"Must doze for a moment."

"All the excitement of the sports you have to deal with has caused you some stress, Zaki dear."

"Must doze."

"But what about finishing the ballet, Zaki?"

She looked at him for an answer, but he was already snoring.

31

"I will accompany you to the boudoir, my lovely lass."

Beth put her hand out and smiled. "I've created a monster," she laughed.

"We're all monsters, my dear."

"Yes, but mine thinks he's a gentleman."

"Music, my dear?"

"Something nice and romantic, Zaki."

"I will turn on the computerized piano, my dear. It will play soft organ music for us that will be simply delightful."

"Yes, soft and soothing."

"May I say you look lovely, my dear?"

"Oh, Zaki, you really are becoming a gentleman."

"All because of you, my darling."

Zaki turned on the computerized piano, switched it to organ and self-play, and hurried back to Beth, who was waiting for him with her arms in the air ready to dance.

"May I, my dear?"

"Certainly, Zaki dear."

They began to dance around the living room, a slow dance with their arms extended and holding each other tight.

"When is your birthday, Zaki?" she finally asked.

"March 25, Beth dear, it's a very important day."

"Why is it important?"

"Well, March 25 is the day some ancient Christian writers believed was the day on which God created the world."

"Oh, really, Zaki, how would they know?"

"I said believed, my dear. It was also thought it was the day on which the fall of Adam took place and the Crucifixion."

"Yes, and what else?"

"According to the ancient writers, the fall of Lucifer and the passing of Israel through the Red Sea occurred on March 25. For centuries, it was even celebrated as New Year's Day in Western culture."

"Why was that, Zaki dear?"

"Because during the Middle Ages, most European countries used March 25 to start the year since it coincided with the coming of spring, a time of rebirth and the planting of new crops. Although January 1 was restored as New Year's Day by 1600, March 25 was still being celebrated as late as 1752 in England and her American colonies."

"Very interesting, Zaki."

"The Church believed the world was created in spring, and that Jesus was conceived and died shortly after the equinox of spring. The Feast of the Annunciation, which is observed on March 25, is thought to be the day the actual incarnation of Jesus as flesh took place in the womb of His mother, Mary. It is celebrated exactly nine months before Christmas Day."

"Wow, and all this from a nice Jewish boy."

"Yes, I was born exactly nine months before Jesus."

"Do you think God knew what he was doing?"

"Of course He did, my dear."

"Yes, of course, Zaki."

"And when is your birthday, Beth dear?"

"June 26."

"Ah, a great day, my dear, it is the birthday of one of the greatest female athletes of all time, Babe Didrikson Zaharias."

"Me and the Babe, Zaki?"

"Yes, my dear, you were born the same day as the Babe."

"I must be pretty good in sports, right, Zaki?"

"If you are anything like your birthday mate, Beth dear, then you are a great athlete."

"What sports do I excel in, Zaki?"

"Well, golf, basketball, and track and field."

"Yes, definitely track and field."

"Well, you're capable of winning Olympic gold medals, my dear."

"Yes, especially track and field."

"Yes, diving and skating and bowling."

"All of them favorites."

"But there's more to your birthday, my dear."

"Yes, who else was born on the day?"

"How about Pearl Buck, the writer who won the 1938 Nobel Prize?"

"Naturally, Zaki."

"Yes, and Peter Lorre and Derek Jeter and the U.S. Army officer who was thought to have invented baseball—"

"All of them geniuses of course."

"Of course, my dear."

"Well, go on, Zaki, I think I can handle it."

"Yes, there's the scientist who devised the temperature scale named after him, Lord Kelvin."

"Another genius—"

"Of the very highest sort—"

Meanwhile, they kept dancing through the room. They plunged and shuffled and circled back from where they had come.

"Oh, tell me more, Zaki dear."

"Well, it's a fabulous day, my dear, with the United Nations charter being signed in San Francisco in 1945 and President Kennedy visiting West Berlin."

"Yes, we told them something, Zaki dear."

"Ich ben ein Berliner."

"Fantastic words—"

"Yes, my dear, I will say them into the Talker device."

She smiled as she danced with Zaki across the room.

"I know them by heart."

"Yes, my dear, they are words worthy of you."

"Independence to all, Zaki dear—"

"But mostly to Madagascar—"

"Why that lovely place, Zaki?"

"Because that is their independence day—"

"Viva la Madagascar!"

"Yes, almost as beautiful as you, my dear."

"Oh, Zaki, you say the sweetest things to me."

"I try my best."

"And your best is good enough for me, Zaki."

"Thank you, Beth dear."

They suddenly stopped dancing and looked at each other. Zaki's huge head threw shadows against the wall.

"Shall we retire to the bedroom, Zaki?"

"I will be most honored."

"You won't push me off the bed again?"

"I have made some changes to my bedroom behavior, my dear."

"Oh, really?"

"Yes, you have taught me well."

"If only I can believe that, my dear Zaki."

"No, really, Beth dear, I will be more agile and less nervous than I have been in the past."

"Like a little pussycat, right, Zaki?"

"Like a tiger, my dear."

"Ooo, Zaki, you're putting chills through my body."

"I will have to warm things up, my dear."

She fell back in his arms, and Zaki caught her without great effort. He then kissed her, and they walked off to the bedroom, Zaki tossing his yellowing handkerchief away behind them.

32

We now come to our Final Quiz question. Zaki Friedman is leading once again as the contestants will write down their final wagers—

The category today is U.S. Presidents—

I will read the final question and then the contestants will write down their answers—

We will give them thirty seconds to come up with the correct answer—

Okay, contestants, here is the final question—

How many U.S. state capitals are named after presidents and name two of the states?

You have thirty seconds—

You have fifteen seconds—

You have ten seconds—

Time's up, contestants, we will reveal your answers—

Let's start with Damon. You had $7,250. Your answer please—

Three, Nebraska and Wisconsin—

No, I'm sorry. The states are correct, but the number of capitals is not—

What did you wager?

Everything, leaving you with nothing—

We come to Cammy, who had $14,750—

What was your answer?

Three, Nebraska and Mississippi—

The two states are correct, but the number of capitals is not—

What did you wager, Cammy?

All but a dollar—

We now come to our champion, Zaki Friedman. Zaki had $22,500 today. Let's see his answer—

Four, Nebraska and Missouri—

Yes, that is the correct answer. The capitals were: Jackson, Mississippi; Jefferson City, Missouri; Lincoln, Nebraska, and Madison, Wisconsin—

Zaki, how much did you wager?

$10,000, giving him a total today of $32,500 and a grand total of $4,125,000—

Unbelievable for a television game show, Zaki, you are number one—

Can anybody beat him? We'll find out if two new contestants tomorrow can finally defeat our champion of champions, Zaki Friedman—

Until then, goodbye everybody!

33

"Let's welcome in Zaki Friedman, all-around genius and answer man extraordinaire."

Zaki stared at the bright lights and tried to smile. "Hello, Jane and Tony, it's good to be here," he finally said.

"You have a new ballet opening, Zaki, how does it feel?"

"Feels great, guys. This ballet has been a dream of mine for quite some time."

"We understand you demonstrate all of the major sports on the stage in this original ballet production."

"Yes, I wrote it myself and composed all of the music."

"That's quite an accomplishment, Zaki, why did you do it?"

Zaki rubbed his bulging cheek and tried to smile once again. "I wanted to write a ballet that incorporated the major sports so women and men could see it together and be equally entertained."

"Yes, great, Zaki, it's something for the entire family," Jane explained.

"The only thing you don't have are the bat boys," Tony added.

"Yes, we thought the stage would be too busy if we incorporated them into the baseball production," Zaki said.

"And what a production it is—"

"--With a rendering of the history of the game, right, Zaki?"

"Yes, we wanted to entertain and explain at the same time."

"To both men and women and their children—"

"It was something I wanted to do, merge sports and dance, and then explain them while entertaining everyone."

"And what about saving the planet, Zaki, is that also something you wanted to do?"

"Well, Jane, I'm only trying to do my part—"

"And what a part it is."

"Yes, Zaki, I believe the water is clearing up with the use of your special Pollution Powder."

"I'm happy that it's working, Jane and Tony. I wanted to help the planet in some way and I think my powder can be used throughout the world to revitalize rivers, lakes, and even the oceans."

"What are you working on next, Zaki?"

"I am really just concentrating on the sports ballet right now."

"And we're sure that is going to be a big hit, too."

"It's something that has never been done before, right, Zaki?"

"It's something new that I hope the people will enjoy."

"And we hear you have something else that's new for the people out there."

"Oh, yes, I almost forgot. I have devised vegetarian and vegan TV dinners for those who can't or don't want to eat meat."

"Bravo, Zaki."

"I was thinking about vegetarians and vegans and thought that they don't even have TV dinners for them. I wanted to do something about it."

"So you'll be marketing these TV dinners yourself, Zaki?"

"I have a lot of help. We have chefs and business people involved in the project and hope to sell a lot of the dinners very soon."

"Another great idea from Zaki Friedman."

"It's getting to be the normal thing to do to expect a great idea from Zaki's very fertile brain."

"When are you going to cure cancer, Zaki?"

"I'm working on that in my laboratory."

"Maybe we'll all live to 150 with Zaki around."

"It's quite possible, Jane and Tony."

"What? 150?"

"Yes, quite possible in the near future."

"Well, that's good news, Zaki."

"Maybe we'll get to see our triple great grandchildren."

"Very possible."

"Zaki as you all know is the all-time champion on 'Pop Quiz.' How's that going?"

"It's been very exciting, Tony."

"You've already made about four million dollars, Zaki."

"I've been thinking about building a house—"

"You could build quite a nice house for that much money."

"And you did it all by answering questions of every sort. How do you know the answers to all these questions, Zaki?"

"I read a lot, Jane. I mean you use everything you've been taught over the years and everything you've read."

"Mind if we try to stump you?"

"No, go right ahead."

"Okay, Zaki, what were the labors of Hercules?"

"You want me to name all twelve labors?"

"Can you do it, Zaki?"

"I'll give it a shot if you want."

"Yes, let's hear what the twelve labors were, Zaki?"

"Well, first he killed the Nemean lion."

"Correct."

"Then he killed the hydra of Lerna. Then he captured the Erymanthian boar. He then captured the hind of Artemis. Then he killed the man-eating Stymphalian birds."

"Yes, very good, Zaki."

"Then he cleaned the Augean stables. He then captured the Cretan bull. He then captured the horses of Diomedes. Next he captured the girdle of Hippolyte, and then captured the cattle of the monster Geryon."

"Great, Zaki."

"He then captured Cerberus, the three-headed dog. And lastly, stole the golden apples of the Hesperides."

"Fantastic, Zaki."

"Yes, that was quite amazing. He got every one of them. Who did he do these labors for, Zaki?"

"That would be his twelve years' service to Eurystheus, king of Mycenae."

"Yes, pretty incredible, Zaki."

"He knows everything, that's for sure."

"Thanks, Jane and Tony, it's my pleasure."

"It's your pleasure to show us how little we know."

"No, it's not like that, Tony. I just answer these questions for the fun of it. I'm not trying to do anything but show that with reading and study, anyone can be smart enough to answer a lot of ridiculous trivia questions."

"And you've made a living doing it—"

"Yes, anything you learn or read over the years can usually be put to some use, Jane. I mean in the course of being on 'Pop Quiz,' I've answered questions that refer to years of education and reading."

"Are you going to put your own book out, Zaki?"

"Yes, I'm in the course of researching it and writing it right now."

"I bet it's a bestseller, Zaki—"

"I sure hope so. It will help fund my inventions and ballets."

"Anything you can tell us about?"

"I can't do anything new right now due to my obligations to the 'Pop Quiz' show and the sports ballet."

"Well, we want you to do well on 'Pop Quiz,' Zaki, so here's another question we came up with. Okay?"

"Fine with me, Jane."

"Okay, here it is, Zaki. This one is going to be tough."

"Fire away."

"What are the Seven Hills of Rome?"

"These are the hills on which Rome was built, Jane. The hills are: the Palatine, the Capitoline, Quirinal, Viminal, Esquiline, Caelian, and Aventine."

"Excellent, Zaki, you named every one of them."

"Thank you."

"You really do know everything."

"I have a very good memory—"

"What were the Oscar nominees for Best Picture in 1937?"

"All of the nominees?"

"Yes, all of them, Zaki—"

"Yes, um, well, there was *The Life of Emile Zola, Lost Horizon, The Good Earth, The Awful Truth, Captains Courageous, Dead End, A Star Is Born, Stage Door, 100 Men and a Girl,* and *In Old Chicago,* and the winner was *The Life of Emile Zola.*"

"That was incredible, truly incredible."

"You didn't think I could do it, Tony?"

"No way, I consider that question just about impossible, Zaki."

"But, you see, it is something I have read through the years."

"You read all the Best Picture nominees?"

"Yes, most of them, Tony—"

"Was it something you were interested in, or you just like to read everything?"

"I happen to be interested in all kinds of trivia and seem to remember everything I come across."

"Simply amazing."

"Zaki is quite astounding in so many ways."

"Thanks very much."

"Well, we couldn't stump him—"

"And I don't think anybody can—"

"Well, let's just hope Zaki begins concentrating on the cause of cancer."

Thunderous applause filled the studio.

"He might be the one to save the human race."

"Thank you, Jane and Tony, it's been my pleasure."

"And our pleasure to be sitting here with you, Zaki—"

"I'll come back and you can ask me some more questions."

"Which we're sure you'll know the answers to—"

"Zaki Friedman, ladies and gentlemen—"

"We'll be back after this—"

34

Welcome to "Pop Quiz"—

Let's meet today's contestants—

A school teacher and avid reader, here's Jill Hallberg—

A lawyer and collector of rare wines, here's James Tifton—

And our champion, who has remained champion for eight straight months and has collected over four million dollars, let's welcome Zaki Friedman—

And now the host of "Pop Quiz," Johnny Jacobs—

Welcome, everybody, to "Pop Quiz," here are today's categories—

Literature, The Human Body, Religion, Myths and Legends, Geography, and Science—

Zaki, our champion, will choose first—

Literature for $200—

The question is, "What was Hiawatha's tribe?"

Zaki—

The Mohawk tribe—

Correct for $200—

It's your choice, Zaki—

Literature for $400—

The question is, "What was the first American novel?"

Zaki—

The Power of Sympathy—

Correct for $400—

Zaki, it's your choice—

Literature for $600—

The question is, "Who was the first woman to win the Pulitzer Prize for fiction?"

Zaki rings in first—
Edith Wharton—
Correct for $600—
Zaki, please choose—
Literature for $800—
The question is, "How many Brothers Karamazov are there?"
Zaki—
There are four—
Correct for $800—
Zaki will choose—
Literature for $1,000—
The question is, "How many sonnets did Shakespeare write?"
Zaki—
154—
Correct for $1,000—
We'll take a break right now so contestants you can all relax—
We'll be back after these messages--

35

Zaki and Beth stood backstage conversing with Blake Warren, director of Zaki Friedman's Sports Ballet. Blake was quite attractive, with flowing blond hair and gleaming blue eyes. He was about a foot taller than Zaki and his svelte figure seemed to emphasize how huge and bulging Zaki's head and face and hands were. None of it was lost on Zaki, who bore no grudge against Blake and actually personally backed him for director of the ballet.

"Do you think it's all going to work out?" Beth was asking.

"I think the ballet will go just fine," Blake replied with an alluring smile. "We just have to make sure the dancers hit their marks."

"You're not nervous, Blake, are you?"

"Nervous? I'm cool as a cucumber."

"See, Zaki?" Beth said, turning toward her diminutive partner. "Blake isn't nervous and he's responsible for the whole show."

"What do you mean he's responsible for the whole show? I wrote the damned thing."

"Yes, but where would we be without someone like Blake?"

"Without someone like Blake?"

"Yes, Zaki, we should be very thankful we found someone who can run the whole operation and make sure the ballet is a success."

"You're giving the credit to Blake, Beth my dear?"

"Well, he deserves some of the credit, Zaki."

Zaki frowned. "Just remember, my dear, who wrote the ballet and who composed all of the music," he finally said. "I'm happy to give credit to others, but first let's see just what kind of director Blake Warren is. I'll be happy to give him some of the credit if all goes well as expected."

"Oh, Zaki, this is a side of you I haven't seen before," Beth replied. "You're really very selfish—"

He watched as she suddenly walked away, not really knowing what he should do. He loved Beth more than anything in the world, but to give away credit to someone who had nothing to do with the writing of the ballet seemed more than generous. This was his production, he told himself. Zaki Friedman's, and no one was going to take it away from him. Not even Beth.

The music began at seven sharp. The curtain went up and the dancers leaped and twirled just as Zaki had imagined. It was a grand show, a great ballet that would be remembered for years. This was a melding of male and female, dance and sports, and no one would go away disappointed. That's exactly how Zaki dreamed it and put it down in words -- a sports ballet for the whole family.

He could see every so often Blake Warren directing the dancers off-stage. He really was doing a great job, Zaki told himself. But to give him half of the credit was ridiculous, ludicrous. He was only doing what Zaki had instructed him to do in the script of the sports ballet. It was all down in black and white and Zaki was the one, the only one, responsible.

He wondered where Beth had wandered to. He wanted to explain to her, reason with her, that he wasn't really selfish, just defensive of his new ballet. He wanted to see it succeed above everything else. He became angry thinking about Beth running off to somewhere when such an important event in his life was taking place. Maybe she was the selfish one, only caring about her own emotions rather than supporting him at this critical time.

The ballet moved along just as he had written it. The baseball portion of the ballet was almost coming to an end. It seemed to him as if the audience had enjoyed it. He couldn't enjoy it anymore, not as long as Beth remained missing. He decided he would go off to look for her. He realized none of it would matter as long as she was not beside him.

"Have you seen Beth?" he asked one of the lighting people before starting on his trek to find her.

"No, no, sir, haven't seen her," he replied.

"Well, she has to be around here somewhere."

He kept walking and looking, past the dancers in their baseball uniforms, and decided he would ask one of the prop people.

"Have you seen Beth Miller?" he asked.

"She was around here somewhere, sir," was the reply.

"Where did you see her last?"

"She was walking toward the offices."

Zaki's bulbous head bobbed among the ropes and dancers. If he wasn't careful, it was just very possible that he might be carted onstage as one of the baseball props. He really wouldn't have realized it until he was bobbing onstage because the only thing he was thinking about was finding Beth.

"Beth dear?" he shouted, peering into one of the empty dressing rooms.

"Beth?"

He kept walking, through the dressing room, until he spotted something near the back. Something or somebody was hidden by lace and chiffon. Zaki bobbed forward, brushing the material aside. He found Beth standing there in Blake Warren's arms.

"Beth?"

The words came out quickly as if a firecracker had suddenly gone off.

"Oh, Zaki, you don't understand—"

"Understand?"

Zaki was confused for a moment, he didn't know what to say, what to do. Should he try to punch Blake Warren in the nose? Should he try to punch Beth Miller in the nose? In the end, he froze for a moment undecided.

"You'll understand some day, my little friend," Blake said, holding on to Beth and grinning. "But, you see, these matters of love are way beyond you right now."

"I'll give you way beyond me, Blake."

"Go away, little man, you couldn't hurt your grandmother. Don't you understand there is a great love here that is beyond your comprehension."

"Comprehension? I'm the smartest person on this planet, Blake."

"Oh, yes, you believe all these things that people are telling you. You actually believe all the nonsense that has been written about you. You're nothing more than a sad little man, Zaki Friedman."

"No, Blake, don't say that," Beth interrupted. "Zaki knows so much—"

"Ah, what does he know?" Blake replied. "Does he know how to satisfy a woman with tender love and care?"

"I thought I did," Zaki shouted. "I thought Beth loved me—"

"Well, you don't know women very well, my little friend. You can answer any question in the world, except how to treat a woman with love and kindness. Yes, Zaki, how do you treat a woman so she never wants to leave?"

Zaki stood there in silence. It was the first question he was ever asked that he didn't really know the answer to. He had an answer in his head, but he began doubting whether it was truly the correct answer.

Instead of answering the question as he always did, Zaki turned around and began walking out the dressing room. He had nothing left to say to either of them, and wondered what his life would be without them. He decided he would go see what was happening with the sports ballet. Blake was finished as far as he was concerned. Let him find another ballet, another play, as long as it wasn't anything to do with him. Let them both find something to do without him. He was done giving charity to inferiors, he would find others to help him.

He walked past the dancers and the sports props and began to snort. He pulled out a clean handkerchief from his pocket and blew his nose. It was the first time he had blown his nose in days.

"Must doze for a moment."

He looked around and went back toward the dressing rooms and the offices. When he found an empty room, he went inside and sat down.

"Must doze."

Zaki tried to fall asleep in the chair but couldn't. He tightened his eyes but still couldn't drift away. Zaki opened his eyes and looked around him. Then he bowed his huge, bulbous head and began to cry.

"Why Beth Miller?" he groaned.

No answer was returned. He wondered whether he should get up and go looking for her once again and then decided against it. She was with Blake Warren, he told himself. How do you love a woman so that she never leaves?

Zaki's head fell forward and he began to cry once again.

36

Zaki stood backstage watching the sports ballet. It was near the ending and Zaki noticed Beth and Blake Warren standing to the side. Blake was giving last-second directions to the dancers, while Beth stood there by his side helping out. Yes, she was standing by his side, Zaki noted. She was standing by his side while Zaki's triumph took place. It was truly an empty victory, Zaki told himself trying not to cry again.

"I'm sorry, Zaki, I really am," said a voice from behind.

Zaki knew exactly who it was. It was Beth, and he slowly turned around to see if he was right.

"You hurt me, Beth Miller," he bitterly said.

"I didn't want to, Zaki, you must believe me."

"But you did," he sniffled. "You broke my heart."

"Your heart will be all right," she replied. "But we were making a mistake."

"A mistake?"

"I loved you for all the wrong reasons, Zaki," she said. "I loved you because you were something I wanted to be."

"You wanted to be me, Beth Miller?"

"I wanted to be the world's smartest person, Zaki. I wanted to stand there and answer all those foolish questions."

"But all I wanted was you, Beth Miller."

"But we were from different worlds, Zaki—"

"Then you do think I'm a monster."

"I think you were right, Zaki, we're all monsters."

"Then why did you want him, Beth Miller?"

She looked down. "Because we are similar, Zaki," she finally said.

"Because he is pretty to look at," he interrupted. "That's the real reason, isn't it?"

She turned, and he grabbed her arm. "Because he was pretty," he said with a frown.

"Maybe I am that shallow, Zaki," she replied. "Maybe so."

She started to walk away, and he sneezed into his yellowing handkerchief. 'Go then," he finally told her. "Go and never come back."

"I'll go," she replied. "I'll pick up my things at the apartment and then you'll never have to see me again."

"But it's your apartment."

"I'll let you have it, Zaki. I'm moving in with Blake."

"Moving in?"

"Yes, we want to be together, Zaki."

Zaki frowned. "You go with Blake, Beth Miller," he growled. "You go with him and I hope I never see you again."

Zaki nudged his oval glasses up the bridge of his nose. He then sneezed once again.

"I think I must doze."

Beth looked at him and frowned. "No dozing, Zaki," she said, putting her hand on his shoulder. "The ballet is almost over. They'll want to see you and applaud you and tell you how much they think of you."

"But it was all because of you, Beth Miller."

"You did it, Zaki. You thought all those wonderful thoughts and answered all of those ridiculous questions. It was you. I only helped get you noticed."

"But we had so many plans, Beth Miller," he whined.

"You don't need me, Zaki, to fulfill your plans."

"But you said you loved me."

"Everything has to end sooner or later, Zaki, don't you understand?"

They could hear the music swelling behind them. The ballet was coming to an end, and they would have to take their place on the stage and thank everyone—

"Because he was pretty," Zaki said, a tear rolling down his bulging cheek. "You only pitied me, Beth Miller."

"I envied you, Zaki," she replied. "You have something not many people have in this world. You can perceive reality and yet, imagine things that never were."

"But I did it just to please you. All those inventions were supposed to impress you and make you love me."

"And they did, but you were thinking up inventions long before I came along. These things that you do you've been doing for quite a long time. I only admired them, Zaki, and I still do."

Then the music swelled once again, wafting backstage and alerting everyone that the ballet had ended.

"Do you think it was a success?" he asked her, not knowing what kind of a response he would get.

"Yes, I do, Zaki, I hope it gives you some happiness—"

He wanted to tell her not to leave, that he would do whatever she asked, when he was suddenly summoned on stage. His huge head bobbed amid the bright lights as he sauntered to the center of the stage. Then he bowed, and someone grabbed his hand. It was Blake Warren. He didn't know what to do, whether to laugh or cry or scream or fight. He then looked over and Beth was walking toward them. She took their hands and also bowed.

Beth stood there smiling as the music faded and the curtain closed. She looked at him, and he didn't know how to react. He could see everyone was smiling, including Blake Warren, and this caused Zaki to finally frown. The minute the curtain closed, Zaki let go of Beth's hand and ran across the stage. He kept running, his huge head bobbing, until he finally reached the wings and sudden darkness. He was away from them, and immediately began to calm down.

"I think I must doze for a moment."

He began looking for a place where he could sit down and doze for a few moments, where he wouldn't be disturbed, when he saw them walking toward him. He knew he must face them, and tried to ready himself.

"Well, the ballet is a smashing success," announced Blake Warren, as he caught a glimpse of Zaki. ""You should thank me, little man."

"You did your job, Blake, and I thank you for that."

"Did my job? I made this piss-ass production something to go home and write about, little man. Don't you forget that—"

"Please, Blake, leave Zaki alone," Beth pleaded, grabbing onto his arm. "He doesn't mean what he says."

"No, I guess not, my pretty little darling," Blake replied with a smile. "He knows he was beaten by the better man. I ended up winning everything, Zaki, your ballet and your woman. I guess you don't have to give me all the credit I deserve."

"I'll tell you what you deserve—"

Zaki reared back and hit Blake in the stomach with his chubby fist. The punch sent Blake bending forward gasping for breath.

"Zaki!" Beth shouted.

"So you want to have a go at me, eh, little man?" Blake finally said. "I'm ready if you are."

"No, stop it!" Beth screamed. "I won't let the two of you kill yourselves over me."

"It really has nothing to do with you, Beth Miller."

"Little man, I should really teach you a lesson," Blake sneered.

"Leave him alone, Blake, you've done enough damage already."

Blake grunted and then pushed Zaki back with a hand to the chest. Zaki went flying back, and then when his enormous head fell back, he landed on the floor.

"You'll pay for this, Blake Warren!" Zaki shouted, his glasses having spun off his face and landing beside him. "I guess I'll have to teach you a lesson, you big oaf."

Zaki was ready to fight, ready to defend his honor, when he realized he couldn't see any longer. He made a worried search for his glasses, all the time promising to get up and settle his score with Blake. After a few moments, his hand discovered his missing glasses, and he stood up prepared to continue the battle.

He stood there, putting his thick, oval glasses back on, when he realized Beth and Blake were gone.

"I must have scared them away," Zaki muttered to himself, straightening his glasses. "They knew when to run."

Zaki frowned, and then realized he was about to snort. He grabbed for his yellowing handkerchief and then sneezed. He rubbed his chest where Blake had pushed him, and then began walking toward the dressing rooms.

He looked for Beth and Blake, but soon realized they had left the building.

37

Welcome to today's second round of "Pop Quiz"—
Louise will select first from one of the categories—
Louise?
Science for $400—
The question is, "How large is the moon?"—
Ranjan—
It is 2,160 miles around—
That's correct, Ranjan, who beat Zaki on the buzzer—
Ranjan, your choice—
Science for $800—
The question is, "How much is the number googol?"
Ranjan, you rang in first—
That number would be 1 followed by 100 zeros—
Very good, you are correct for $800—
Ranjan, please choose—
Science for $1200—
The question is, "Which is harder, topaz, quartz, or corundum?"
Zaki—
That would be quartz—
No, I'm sorry, Zaki, that is incorrect—
Ranjan—
I will have to say corundum—
Yes, that is the correct answer—
Well, ladies and gentlemen, we have witnessed something today—
Zaki Friedman has missed a question—
Ranjan, it is your selection—
Science for $1600—

The question is, "On the periodic table, W is the symbol for Wolfram, which is also known as what?"

Ranjan?

Vanadium?

No, that is incorrect—

Zaki, what is the answer?

I would have to say Tungsten--

And that is correct, Zaki—

Zaki, your choice—

Let's finish the category, Science for $2000—

The question is, "How long is a cosmic year?"

Zaki?

It is approximately 225 million earth years—

Yes, that is correct for $2000—

Well, we had an interesting thing happen just a few minutes ago, ladies and gentlemen, but now it seems everything has returned to normal—

But you never know what could happen so I'd advise everyone to stick around—

We'll be back after these messages—

38

Zaki was still trying to get over Beth leaving him. It had been days, weeks, since he had emerged from the apartment she had left him. He had no intention of ever going out again. He decided he would stay inside and invent. Do anything but talk to human beings again. They had no logic, Zaki told himself, they just walked around and tried to hurt the next guy or gal they could find. It was all so ridiculous.

All he wanted to do was invent, invent something so miraculous people would gasp. He had no idea how long it had taken, but he finally came up with something he called, The Thinking Cap. It was a computerized microprocessor that sat on the person's head and helped that person think. That's all it was meant to do, just help the person think about what he wanted to think about.

The first subject Zaki thought about was chemistry. He thought about the chemical elements and kept on thinking.

"What about cancer?" he finally asked the Thinking Cap.

The Thinking Cap beeped and buzzed and lights went on and off. Zaki sat there, hunched over, thinking about the causes of cancer.

"Abnormal growth of cells," he repeated, as the suggestion coursed through his brain. "There must be an acceptable pH balance of the skin—"

Zaki smiled. "Yes, yes, an acceptable pH balance," he muttered to himself. "The skin usually being somewhat alkaline in nature when attacked by cancer."

Zaki sat there thinking about how to cure cancer. The Thinking Cap, meanwhile, beeped and buzzed and sent thought currents and suggestions into Zaki's brain.

"Cancer usually attacks older skin, dry and alkaline in nature," Zaki mumbled to himself. "One must think about using some sort of acidic solution or lotion to rid the skin of the dryness and the abnormal cells."

Zaki sat there thinking and then decided it was time to go to sleep. The stress of trying to come up with a cure for cancer was just a little too much for him.

"I think I must doze for a moment."

He reached up and unstrapped the Thinking Cap from his head. It was still beeping and buzzing as he placed it in his lap.

"This might be too good for people," he said to himself about the Thinking Cap. "I don't think I want everybody walking around thinking up great thoughts. I don't know whether I'll ever make one of these babies available to the public. It just wouldn't be right."

He sat there with the Thinking Cap in his lap and let his huge head fall backwards. Zaki was soon snoring.

He slept for a while until the Thinking Cap made some sort of shrill beep and he opened his eyes. The Cap was still in his lap, beeping and buzzing with lights going on and off and blinking every so often.

"I don't know if I can really shut this thing off," Zaki told himself. "I wonder what shutting it off would do to the microprocessor?"

The nap had somewhat revived him, and he decided to put the Thinking Cap back on his head. "Curing cancer must take into consideration the pH balance of the skin and body—"

The Thinking Cap was still concentrating on how to cure cancer. The whole process of thought had become fascinating to Zaki. It seemed the possibilities were endless in using the Thinking Cap.

"There must be some sort of replacement of the abnormal cells," he mumbled in rhythm with the thoughts being sent by the Thinking Cap. "These cells must be replaced by normal cells in some sort of process using rays or beams."

The Thinking Cap was mesmerizing. Its only mission was to resolve any problem one might have with a solution of some kind, whether or not the solution was realistic or not.

"So then a replacement ray or beam or gene therapy must be invented to destroy the abnormal cells and replace them with normal cells," he mumbled to himself. "This is one way in which the cancer is destroyed."

"The other way would be an acidic solution of some kind to regenerate the skin and destroy the abnormal cells, the skin being aged and alkaline."

Zaki smiled and took off the Thinking Cap. It was still beeping for some reason. He placed the Thinking Cap down in a corner of the room, and then thought to himself the ways to cure cancer as suggested by the Thinking Cap. If one of the methods should work, he would be the most respected scientist in years, maybe centuries. He knew the one who cured cancer would make millions.

"Maybe I'll start on some replacement ray tomorrow," he said to himself, sitting down once again, "although it might be quicker to test an acidic solution of some kind or skin genes that can be injected into the body."

He snorted into his yellowing handkerchief and sighed. He had plenty of time to fool around with some cure, he told himself. In the meantime, he wanted to create a great symphony of some kind. He stood up and retrieved the computerized violin. He then bent down and grabbed the Thinking Cap. He would put the Thinking Cap on and then with the computerized violin in his hands, would create some great symphony.

The Thinking Cap buzzed and beeped as he thought about the symphony. Lights flashed on and off.

"The symphony should have verses and a chorus and a break of some kind," he mumbled while the Thinking Cap beeped and whirred. "It should be constructed along the lines of any conventional song with recurring themes and riffs."

He began playing the computerized violin as the Thinking Cap's lights danced above his head. He hit upon a riff of some kind and pressed a button. The computerized violin played the music accompanied by horns, flutes, and percussion. It was a symphony of thought.

Yes, that was what he would call it, he mused -- The Thought Symphony. He listened to the music swelling across the room. It sounded like a summer's day, or the beginning of spring. Yes, that was the Thought Symphony, a tribute to Nature and life. It reverberated through the room.

"I wonder how it would sound with some oboes and clarinets," he said to himself as the Thinking Cap lights sparkled. "Maybe I should play it on the computerized piano? That would probably be a very stimulating sound."

Zaki sneezed and searched around for a clean handkerchief. There were many handkerchiefs littering the floor since he had not bothered to wash any of them, and no one had visited him since Beth had left. Zaki finally reached down and picked up one of the multi-colored handkerchiefs lying on the floor, He snorted into it and threw it back down to the carpet.

Zaki kept humming the tune to the Thought Symphony. He picked up the computerized violin and pressed a button on top. In a few moments, a huge sheet of music with the appropriate notes written out appeared from one of the slots. He now had a typed copy of the Thought Symphony.

"This will sell millions," he said to himself. "Now I've just got to take it to the agent's office. Oh, where is Beth Miller? She always did that for me. I really do need that woman. I wonder when she is coming back."

He paused for a moment, and then began to cry. He cried and howled and then he sniffled and snorted.

"But she's never coming back," he mumbled to himself. "She's never coming back and I'm never going out again. They will find me and the Thought Symphony when the time comes. In the meantime, I will take a shower-bath."

He grumbled for a moment, and then stripped off his clothing, leaving each item on the floor. When he was naked, he kept walking toward the bathroom.

"She will come back to me," he sang as loud as he could. "She will come back and we will be in love again. Do you hear me? We will be in love again. Yes, love."

Zaki took off his huge, oval glasses and stepped into the bathtub. He turned on the water and sighed. He sat down in the tub and then turned on the shower. He always took a bath this way. He always described it as being in paradise for a short time. The shower was like a refreshing waterfall tumbling into a clear pool of water. Yes, that was the way Zaki thought about it. It was like sitting in a pool of water as an energizing blast of water sizzled from above. It was definitely like paradise.

Zaki sat in the spray of water and tried to decide what he would do next. There was an invention he was still working on and wanted to test. It was called, the Book Maker, and if it worked the way Zaki had planned, it would generate books just by feeding it plots and dialogue lines. It would be the greatest shortcut to writing a serious novel.

"Zaki refreshed," he told himself, shutting off the water. He reached down and grabbed his glasses, and then picked up a towel.

After putting on his old clothes once again, Zaki made the trek across the apartment. He reached down and retrieved a yellowing handkerchief and snorted into it. He then threw it back down to the floor.

"I will work on the Book Maker," he mumbled to himself. "I wonder what the Thinking Cap will have to say about it."

The Book Maker was a small screen in which one added elements of the book he wished to write. The Book Maker then did the rest, finishing a full-length novel in a few days. Zaki was working on something involving his theory of the universe. He had fed the invention his notes on the planets and science and a few comments he would like to make. The Book Maker did the rest. Zaki's book was already half-finished, something that would normally have taken months.

"Yes, the sun was still relatively young," he mumbled as the Thinking Cap buzzed and beeped on his head. "You might make some statements as to the possibility of life elsewhere in the universe."

Zaki turned on the microphone attached to the Book Maker screen. He began dictating his ideas and the Thinking Cap's suggestions. The Book Maker took the suggestions and put them into words and sentences. Pages of the book flew by as the Book Maker worked on.

This was going to be a revolutionary new way to write a book. Most books took months and years to complete, but not books written on the Book Maker. One could dictate a whole novel or leave it to the Book Maker to compose most of the sentences. The ideas were generated by the writer and the writing was completed by the machine. It saved time and unnecessary work. In only a few days, one could have a completed volume and then try to get that sold or move on to a new idea. It made life a lot easier for everybody. The completed manuscript could then be sent off to another screen somewhere else, preferably to an agent, and the whole process could begin again.

"The book is almost completed," Zaki muttered with the Thinking Cap still blinking above. "I think we have incorporated most of the ideas and suggestions."

"You have not described your idea of life elsewhere and what that life would be like," Zaki suddenly mumbled, prompted by the blinking Thinking Cap on his head. "You may want to warn people how dangerous it would be to interact with intelligent alien life and suggest they may be carrying some mysterious diseases of some sort."

Zaki tried to smile. "Yes, the Thinking Cap is definitely correct," he said to himself. "I will give my ideas on intelligent alien life and dissuade people from trying to interact with them."

He began dictating his thoughts into the Book Maker microphone and it hummed in response. The pages were being filled as Zaki droned on about intelligent life elsewhere in the universe.

"They may, of course, be even humanlike in appearance," he noted. "That does not mean they believe in general human values."

Zaki kept dictating into the Book Maker microphone. The book was almost completed. It had only taken a few days.

"When I'm finished with this," he noted to himself, "I will start on my autobiography. That will be something the people will enjoy reading."

He grunted and snorted as the inventions hummed and beeped in reply. He then picked up one of the yellowing handkerchiefs lying on the floor and sneezed.

39

Welcome to our Final Quiz question. This is the last game before our college tournament which will begin next week. Zaki and his challengers will be off for a month because after the college tournament we will have our teen tournament, which will continue for two weeks—

Okay, contestants, you have all written down your wagers and now we will reveal the final question—

You will have thirty seconds to write down your answers—

Here is the final question for today's "Pop Quiz"—

The category is Mythology—

In Norse mythology, who was the god of agriculture, sun and rain?—

Fifteen seconds—

Ten seconds—

Five seconds—

Time's up, contestants—

We come first to Alice, who was in third place. What was your answer?—

Loki is incorrect. How much did you wager? Everything, leaving you with nothing. I'm very sorry—

Let's see what Kerrick put down—

Balder is incorrect. You had $11,000. How much did you bet? $10,999, leaving you with one dollar.

So we come to our champion, Zaki Friedman. Did he have the correct answer?--

Freyr is correct. Unbelievable, Zaki, you've done it again. How much did you wager? $15,000, giving you a total of $53,000. Fantastic—

Zaki has now earned more than five million dollars on "Pop Quiz." Truly unbelievable. Well, there are more games to be played and everyone wants to see how long Zaki can remain champion. So join us for our next game and until then, good-bye everybody!

40

Zaki was watching television. He was watching himself on "Pop Quiz," resolving not to go back to the studio when the special tournaments ended. He was about to press the remote and change the channel when the doorbell rang.

"Hi, Zaki dear," said someone from behind the door. It was Jeremiah, and Zaki hurried to open the door.

"Hello, Jerry, how are you?" he said, motioning for his brother to come inside.

"Wow, this place is now a dump, my intellectual sibling. Where the heck is Sweet Brown Eyes?"

"She left me, Jerry, to be with that director."

"It's pretty obvious, my intelligent older brother. How long have you been here without her?"

"Oh, a few weeks and I don't think I'm ever coming out again."

Jeremiah shook his head, and headed for the couch. He stepped around the discarded handkerchiefs and the dirty underwear and sat down watching whatever was on the television screen.

"You won again?" he finally asked.

Zaki nodded his huge head. "More than five million dollars, Jerry," he said.

Jeremiah whistled. "That's a lot of loot, bro," he said. "Maybe it's time you bought yourself a house and got the hell out of here."

Zaki frowned. "I'm not leaving without her, my young brother," he snorted. "I have a feeling she'll be coming back."

Jeremiah looked at him and shook his head. "She took all of her things?" he asked.

Zaki nodded.

"The guy, that director, he's very good looking?"

Zaki nodded again.

"You caught them kissing?"

Zaki nodded once again.

"Hello, my intellectual bro, reality calling," Jeremiah sang.

"But she told me she loved me—"

"And maybe she does, but her love might not be the same as your love. Understand, bro?"

"But she told me she loved me."

"Yes, and she meant it at the time, but things have changed."

"I never should have hired that Blake Warren to be director of the sports ballet," he moaned.

"You hired some good looking bozo to be the director, bro? Are you crazy?"

"What do you mean?"

"Why these good looking directors are lady magnets, Zaki. I've seen it all the time. A guy thinks things are going well with his girl and then invites a good looking friend or colleague to meet her and then, zazoom, he finds her running off with the guy to some town in France. Happens all the time."

"But she said I was going to be the greatest genius of all time."

"And she did her part to make you famous, my intellectual bro, but these babes with brown eyes they're looking for some stud to satisfy them."

"I thought I satisfied her."

Jeremiah nodded. "Yeah, maybe you did, bro," he said. "You want to pass the chips?"

"But you don't understand, Jerry, I'm not leaving this apartment until she returns to me."

"I hope you have a lot of clean underwear, Zaki."

"She'll be back."

"How about if we get our minds off Miss Sweet Eyes and watch the football game? I want you to study some of the statistics, Zaki."

"But why?"

"Because I want to make a bet, bro, got it? I'm not going to sit here with you and cry about some babe who's flown the coop. I want to make some extra money."

"Bet on New York all the way, my young bro."

"Giving the points?"

"Yeah, they're going to demolish the opposition."

"Well, get on the computer and check it out, Zaki. I don't want to lose today and you haven't exactly been on a hot streak."

"Because Beth Miller left?"

"Yeah, you lost Miss Sweet Eyes and you also missed a question on 'Pop Quiz.' You don't think I watch television?"

"It was because I was distracted, my young bro."

"Okay let me see if you have any magic left, Zaki."

"Give me the toughest one you have, Jerry."

"How about women's basketball?"

"Give it a shot, Jer."

"Who was the WNBA champion in 2003?"

"That would be the Detroit Shock."

"Who was the WNBA rookie of the year in 1998?"

"Rookie of the year, Jer?"

"You want some time to think about it?"

"No, it's Tracy Reid of Charlotte."

"Okay, but I think we better stick to football."

"Shoot."

"Super Bowl ten?"

"Pittsburgh 21, Dallas 17."

"Super Bowl MVP in 1971?"

"Chuck Howley of Dallas."

"Number one NFL draft choice in 1945?"

"Charley Trippi of Georgia by the Chicago Cards."

"All right, everything seems to be working normally, my genius bro. Now what do you think about New England giving six and a half points?

"Give the points, Jerry, and sit back and get rich quick."

"Yes, you seem to be all right, my intellectual sibling."

"Well, what's next?"

"Turn on the game, Zaki, that's all that's left."

"But, of course, my young bro."

Zaki turned on the football game and then put the remote down on the coffee table. "Chips or popcorn?" he finally asked.

"You know I always prefer chips, Zaki dear. How about some dip?"

"You can't have everything, Jer."

"Well, sit down and enjoy the game, Zaki, it's going to be about three hours."

"I'm going to take care of some business, Jerry."

"You're going to try to contact Miss Sweet Eyes?"

Zaki frowned. "No, I'm going to try to forget her and move on."

"Now you're talking, Zaki boy. There's no use to letting some dame interrupt your life."

"But she wasn't some dame, Jerry. She was the love of my life."

"Now let's not be too hasty, my genius bro. You don't have too much experience with the chicks, you know."

"I have enough, Jerry, to know—"

"Touchdown!"

Zaki watched as Jeremiah began running around the apartment shouting with a fist in the air.

"I told you to give the points, my young bro."

He bent down and kissed Zaki's enormous head. "You still have your magic, Zaki boy. I don't know why I ever doubted you."

"Because Beth Miller left me."

"What?"

"You thought I had lost my magic because Beth Miller left me."

"Oh, yeah, right."

"But New York scored, anyway."

Jeremiah smiled. "Yes, Zaki, my dear, you still know what you're talking about. Why I'm never going to doubt you again."

"Well, you know, Jerry, it wasn't hard—"

"Oh, crap!"

"An interception and he's bringing it all the way back."

"Damn."

"Don't worry, Jerry, New York will win the game today."

"Who was the NFL Rookie of the Year in 1967?"

"Mel Farr of Detroit. You don't think I've lost my magic again, do you?"

"You can never tell, Zaki boy. One missed question on 'Pop Quiz' and then who knows what will happen?"

"Better give me another one."

"Okay, who led the AFL in scoring in 1960?"

"Gene Mingo of Denver."

"Yes, it looks good."

"You think I got my magic back, Jerry?"

"Probably, Zaki dear, but you can never tell for sure."

"Well, you sit and watch the game and I think you're going to like the results."

"I can't afford to lose this game, Zaki dear."

"It's only money, my young bro. Anyway, it's only the beginning of the second quarter."

Zaki began walking away, uninterested in the football game, when he looked back at Jeremiah.

"New York's on the twenty yard line, Zaki."

"I told you they were a sure thing, my young bro."

It was about a half hour later that Jeremiah realized Zaki had not returned to watch the game. He wondered what his genius of a brother was doing. What was so much more important than the football game?

"Zaki?"

He began walking around the apartment trying to find him when he noticed somebody standing near the window.

"Zaki, what the heck are you doing?"

He noticed Zaki was holding something in front of his eyes. One of his inventions, no doubt.

"What is that thing, Zaki?"

"The View Finder," was the response.

"Well, what the hell is the View Finder, Zaki?"

"I'm watching some girl in the other building."

"Is she walking around nude?"

"No, just walking around."

"Is she in her bra and panties?"

"No, just standing there in the living room."

"Well, what the hell is so fascinating about that?"

"Well, the View Finder makes everything fascinating, Jer."

"Yeah, how?"

"Well, it's like those machines at the airport."

"What machines?"

"You know the scanning machines that reveal everything—"

Jeremiah smiled. "You mean those machines that show everybody without their clothes on?"

Zaki nodded. "It's the same technology I used for the View Finder."

"Damn, let me see, Zaki."

Zaki handed Jeremiah the View Finder and he put it in front of his eyes. In the building across from them, a blond woman was walking around naked.

"Holy Cow, Zaki! These things are the best thing you ever invented! Geez, what a view! It's like she isn't wearing anything at all!"

"The scanning ray goes right through the clothing—"

"Holy Cow!"

"Jerry, don't get too excited—"

"Excited? I'm as excited as I'll ever get!"

"Do you think people will buy them, Jer?"

"Buy them? They'll buy you if you don't watch out."

"I'm selling them on my website—"

Jeremiah lowered the View Finder. "Selling them, are you out of your mind?"

"They're just one of my inventions."

"This is not just an invention, Zaki. No, this is the mother lode. God forgive me, not the mother lode but the top of the mountain. Make that top of the mountains. Geez, Zaki, these things are unbelievable. You can't just sell them like a TV set or a cell phone. You can see everything with these things and I mean everything."

"What about the football game?"

"What football game?"

"You mean you see one little female and everything else goes out the window?"

"You better hope I don't throw you out the window and keep these glasses for myself."

Zaki hissed at Jeremiah's comment. He always laughed when Jeremiah was around.

"I'll give you a pair if you help me clean up the apartment, Jer."

"No, suddenly I'm in the mood for a nice, long stroll. You know what I mean?"

"You want to look at everybody, Jer?"

"Why the hell not? It's the most interesting thing I can think of."

"But what about the game?"

"I gave the points, Zaki."

"Then you don't think I've lost my magic, my young bro?"

"Magic? Magic? Why you're the most magical guy I've ever known, Zaki. Anyone who can cook up something like this View Finder is more than a genius. Why he's a true American hero."

"You really think so?"

"I'm ready to build a statue of you myself."

"Should I pose?"

"Not while I'm wearing the View Finder, Zaki, that's really gross."

Jeremiah started walking to the door holding the View Finder in front of him.

"But I haven't been out in a long time, Jerry."

"So you were in and now you're out, what's the big deal?"

"The big deal is I vowed not to leave until she came back."

"You planned on growing old in here?"

"But she has to come back."

"Why? There's some law that you know of that says she has to come back, Zaki?"

"But she'll get tired of Blake Warren."

"How long is that going to take, Zaki dear? I say let's go out and have some fun and start living. That's the only way she might come back. If she finds out that you're having a good time without her, she might get jealous and come back. Now that's a possibility."

"You think so, Jer?"

"You know these chicks, Zaki boy. They want to be where the action is. If you become the action, then it figures that she might come back to you."

"I never figured it that way before."

"Oh, yeah, these dames like to play it real cool. They know if you're having fun without them."

"Then let's go out and have some fun, Jerry."

"I couldn't have said it better myself, my intellectual sibling."

They marched toward the door, opened it, and Zaki hesitantly stepped out. Jeremiah followed wearing the View Finder glasses.

"Behind me, Zaki, stay behind me. I'm wearing the View Finder, for heaven's sake, and I have no intention of seeing my older brother's naked butt."

Zaki hissed and snorted, and then he let Jeremiah get in front of him. "I don't know whether I should go, Jerry."

"I told you she's going to know if you're having fun."

"Okay, okay, I'll listen to you for a change."

They walked down the empty corridor and headed for the elevator.

"Aren't there people in this building?" Jeremiah complained.

"Everybody's watching the game, Jerry."

"Oh, yeah, the game. Well, there are more important things, you know."

"Like using the View Finder—"

"I'll let you know in a little while."

Zaki laughed and they marched into the waiting empty elevator.

41

The elevator doors opened and Jeremiah was suddenly in paradise. The lobby was crowded with men and women, especially women.

"Holy Cow!" Jeremiah whispered. "This is really obscene, Zaki. You are an American hero."

"One big nudist camp, right, Jerry?" Zaki snorted.

"What's the state tree of Maryland?"

Zaki turned his head and saw a tall woman with blond hair standing there. "I beg your pardon?" he replied.

"You're Zaki Friedman, I saw you on 'Pop Quiz.'"

Zaki could see Jeremiah sticking his tongue out from behind. He was getting embarrassed knowing that Jeremiah was seeing what she looked like in her birthday suit. The woman turned and suddenly noticed Jeremiah and the View Finder behind her.

"You're taping this?" she asked.

"Oh, yes, yes," Zaki stuttered. "You don't mind, do you?"

The woman shook her head. "Not at all," she grinned. "Do I get any money?"

"We'll send it to you," Zaki huffed.

"What about the state tree of Maryland?" the woman asked.

"The white oak," Zaki replied.

"You are one of a kind," the woman smiled, shaking her head.

"Thank you," Zaki said, as the woman walked away.

"One of a kind nothing," Jeremiah was saying from behind the View Finder. "That was the nicest caboose I've ever seen."

"I hope nobody realizes what you're really doing, my young bro."

"It's worth the risk, Zaki, it's truly worth the risk."

He watched as Jeremiah moved the View Finder from right to left. "The world has become one big candy store, Zaki," he said. "I thank you from the bottom of my heart."

"Maybe I shouldn't put these things up for sale," Zaki mumbled. "Let's go back to the apartment, Jerry."

"No, I want you to have some fun, Zaki, and that's what we're going to do."

They walked across the lobby, Jeremiah panting and laughing, and out the front doors.

"This city has new meaning for me, Zaki boy."

"Why?"

"Wouldn't you like to know," Jeremiah laughed. "I'll take four thousand, Zaki."

"Four thousand what?"

"Four thousand View Finders and don't bother to wrap them," Jeremiah hissed from behind the View Finder.

"I'd better take them off my website," Zaki sighed. "Let's go back to the apartment, Jerry."

"Not on your life, Zaki dear. I'm just getting the hang of this thing."

They were walking down the sidewalk when some girls and guys walking in the other direction stopped them.

"What group has the top-selling album of all time?" asked one of the girls.

"You're that genius from TV," said another girl.

"Yes, thank you, ladies and gents," Zaki replied. "The answer is the Eagles."

"Ask him something hard," said one of the guys.

"Okay, genius geek, who was Miss America in 1971?"

The guy who asked the question began to laugh. "Do you watch pretty girls, genius geek?" he said.

The girls began laughing, too, and surrounded Zaki and Jeremiah. They noticed Jeremiah holding the View Finder in front of his face.

"What's he doing?" asked one of the girls.

"Pictures, ladies, just pictures," Zaki explained.

"Yeah, pictures," Jeremiah wheezed.

"Well, what's the answer, genius geek?"

"I would have to say Phyllis Ann George," Zaki finally answered.

The guy who asked the question laughed. "This genius geek is out of his mind," he said. "He knows everything about everything. Geez, who would remember who the freaking Miss America was?"

"I read a lot," Zaki replied.

"Oh, you read a lot," the guy repeated. "He reads a lot."

"Boy, you have the biggest head I've ever seen," said one of the girls. She noticed Jeremiah standing there in front of her with the View Finder on his face.

"Hello, baby," he hissed.

"Hey, what the hell are you doing, bozo," one of the girls shouted.

"Taking our pictures nothing, that's some kind of device of some kind."

"I bet he can see our panties or something."

The girls began to scream causing Jeremiah and Zaki to begin running down the street. When the guys suddenly realized what was going on, they began to chase after them.

"Get that camera!" one of the girls shouted.

Jeremiah and Zaki scrambled around the corner and hid in a nearby alleyway. Jeremiah was now holding the View Finder in his hands.

"Don't let them find us, Zaki," he hooted. "This is the greatest invention in the history of the world!"

"They're going to kill us when they catch us, Jerry. We better follow this alleyway away from here."

They hurried down one of the passages and found themselves back on the street. Jeremiah put the View Finder under his shirt as they walked back toward the apartment.

"Oh, look at those beautiful women," Jeremiah moaned. "If I could only use the View Finder."

"Don't let anyone see it, Jerry," Zaki snorted. "We have to get back to the apartment."

They were hurrying away, trying not to let anyone see them, when two couples blocked their way.

"You're Zaki Friedman," one of the guys said.

"Yes, you're that genius on TV," said one of the women.

"How can I help you?" Zaki replied.

"Come on, Zaki, we've got no time to play around," Jeremiah said.

"Wait a minute, I've got a question for you," said one of the men.

"Okay, but hurry, sir," Zaki replied.

"Who was the NCAA Division I Lacrosse champion in 1983?" the man asked with a smile.

"Men or women?" Zaki said.

"Both," the man said with another smile.

"Come on, Zaki, we've got to go," Jeremiah urged.

"Just a minute, my young bro."

"Well, what's the answer?" the other man said with a smile.

"Syracuse and Delaware," Zaki finally answered. "Now if you will excuse us—"

"What's the trick?" one of the men asked. "You have some electronic device on you?"

"That's what it is," the other man agreed. "Probably on his cell phone."

"Well, he doesn't have anything on TV," one of the women argued.

"Anything that you know about it," one of the men shot back.

Meanwhile, Zaki and Jeremiah hurried down the avenue. After a few moments, Zaki stopped hurrying.

"I think I must doze for a moment," he said out of breath.

"No dozing, Zaki," Jeremiah said. "Those guys are still trying to hunt us down."

"I knew I shouldn't have left the apartment."

"Well, I have no regrets. Those girls were unbelievable, Zaki."

"Yeah, and wait until their boyfriends find us."

As soon as the words came out of Zaki's mouth, the guys who were chasing them suddenly spotted them.

"Hey, there they are!" one of the guys shouted.

Zaki and Jeremiah began to run. They ran down the sidewalk, hoping they could reach the door of the apartment building before they were caught from behind and pummeled to a pulp.

They had almost made it when one of the guys suddenly leaped on top of them. Zaki fell to the pavement with a thud. Another guy caught Jeremiah and pushed him to the ground.

"So you were looking at their panties, huh?" one of the guys said.

"No, no, I didn't see any panties," Jeremiah said.

"I bet," another of the guys growled.

"Give me that thing under your shirt," one of the guys demanded.

Jeremiah took the View Finder out and handed it over to one of the guys. He began breaking it on a nearby wall.

"No, no, it can't be, it was such a lovely invention," Jeremiah moaned.

"Invention? Who invented it? The genius geek?"

"It was not meant to be used by a lot of people," Zaki said, lying on the ground, his huge head on the pavement.

"Yeah, right," one of the guys said. "Perverts."

"You wouldn't say that if you saw what I saw," Jeremiah said.

"Yeah, and what did you see?"

"How pretty your girlfriends are," Jeremiah replied.

"That's it."

The guys proceeded to punch and hit Zaki and Jeremiah until they were bruised and bloodied.

"That will teach you guys a lesson," one of them said as they ran away.

"Jerry, are you all right?" Zaki asked.

"My poor, poor View Finder, smashed to pieces," Jeremiah groaned.

"Let's go back to the apartment, Jerry."

"Pieces, pieces," Jeremiah continued to groan.

Zaki stood up and saw the View Finder in pieces near the wall. He looked at Jeremiah, who still refused to get off the ground.

"But you don't understand, Zaki," he moaned. "That was the best thing I ever had in my entire life. Oh, the tragedy of it all."

"I have more of them, my young bro."

"More of them?"

Jeremiah bounced up from the ground with a smile. "More of them, Zaki?" he grinned.

Zaki nodded his head, and slowly walked back to the apartment. Jeremiah, still grinning, did a small dance behind him.

42

Welcome to Pop Quiz—
Here are today's contestants—
A teacher and ballroom dancing fan, let's meet Jackie Wright—
A lawyer and art collector, here's Thomas Logan—
And our returning champion, who hasn't lost in months, let's say hello again to Zaki Friedman—
Now here's the host of Pop Quiz, Johnny Jacobs—
Hello, players, let's look at today's categories—
We have America, Science, Literature, Geography, Astronomy, and Sayings—
Zaki, our longtime champion, will choose first. Zaki?
America for $200—
What state is home to Bacon, Looneyville, and Wink?—
Zaki?
I will say Texas—
You will be correct—
Zaki, please choose—
America for $400—
What state is the home to Roachtown, Fishhook, and Normal?—
Zaki?
I'll say Illinois—
You are correct—
Please select—
Literature for $600—
Who invented the word "assassination?"—
Zaki—
Shakespeare—

Correct for $600—
America for $600—
What is the state musical instrument in South Dakota?—
Zaki?
The fiddle—
Yes, the fiddle would be correct—
Zaki, it's your choice—
America for $800—
By what name was Washington, D.C. known in 1791?—
Zaki—
I think that was Federal City—
Correct for $800—
We'll take a short break and then we'll be back, ladies and gentlemen,
so stick around—

43

"We have with us today, Zaki Friedman, the all-around genius who has won more than five million dollars on 'Pop Quiz' and has come up with cures for the common cold and cancer and inventions to help the planet. Welcome, Zaki—"

"It's my pleasure to be with you today, Megan."

Zaki sat there on the set, his enormous head filling the television camera monitor. He crossed his legs and tried to smile, attempting to hide his inner dislike for interviews and television.

"You have won more than five million dollars on 'Pop Quiz.' How did you do it?"

"By knowing the answers to all those questions, Megan," he replied.

"How do you know all the answers, Zaki, is there a trick to it like many people are saying?"

"There's no trick to it, Megan, I just read a lot and have come across the answers to all these questions at some time during my readings."

"You know some people say you have some electronic device on you that relays the answers to your ear. What do you say about that?"

"No device, Megan. I really do know the answers to all these questions. I don't even have such a device in my laboratory. I never invented one, I can tell you that."

"Well, some people say it is impossible for anyone to know as much as you do. That no one can answer all those questions—"

Zaki shifted in his seat. He knew he was going to be asked about electronic devices and the answers to all those ridiculous questions.

"You know it's like what Immanuel Kant said about things we are born with, things we learn and things we learn from experience. These are the bits of knowledge and information that sets us apart from one another. In some way, I was born with a good imagination. This imagination helped me in learning in school and then learning in the world. It was a melding of imagination and reality that I used to gain much information about the world."

"Then you do know the answers to all those questions. You're not cheating in any way?"

"No, I would never cheat, Megan. I think anyone who tried to cheat would be caught very easily. There would be physical evidence of some kind. No, I don't need to cheat. I have come across the information in those questions many times during my lifetime. There are very few questions I don't know the answer to."

"I'm very glad you said that, Zaki, because we have a surprise guest with us today who says you don't know the answers to a lot of questions and he will prove it to all of us."

Zaki shifted in his seat and snorted into his handkerchief. He was never told about any surprise guest being on the show.

"Who is this surprise guest?" he finally asked. "Do I know him?"

Megan smiled. "Yes, of course, you know him, Zaki," she said. "And we'll bring him out in a second."

Zaki thought about who it could be. Names began circulating in his head, everything from Beth Miller to Jeremiah.

"Bring out the surprise guest, Megan. I have a right to know who it is."

He could see Megan grinning, something like the look of a cat after catching the canary.

"Okay, let's bring him out. Let's say hello to Blake Warren, the director of Zaki's Sports Ballet."

"Blake Warren?" Zaki shouted.

He watched as the handsome blond director who stole his woman sauntered across the stage. He waved to the crowd and then sat down on the other side of Megan, across from Zaki.

"Hello, everyone," Blake said with a smile. "Hello, little man."

Zaki frowned upon hearing the words. He suddenly knew this was a set-up of some kind to make him look bad in front of a lot of people.

"Hello, moron," Zaki replied.

"Now, please, you two," Megan interrupted.

"He is just upset because I am his worst nightmare," Blake laughed. "Today you will see how much Zaki Friedman doesn't know."

"Well, it's not going to be because of your brain," Zaki shouted back.

"We'll just see about that," Blake said.

"Okay, okay, let's get to it," Megan said. "Blake says he has questions no one, including Zaki Friedman, can answer. Isn't that true, Blake?"

"That's very true, Megan. I want to ask Zaki Friedman in front of this huge television audience questions he can't answer no matter how hard he cheats."

"Cheats?" Zaki roared. "I never cheated in my life."

"How about it, Zaki?"

"Fire away, you Neanderthal."

"Okay."

The small audience that had come to the taping had gotten quiet. Everybody was wondering just what would actually happen.

"How did the universe begin, Zaki?"

Blake Warren wore an evil grin as he watched Zaki's reaction. He noticed that Zaki was temporarily stunned by the question.

"How did the universe begin?" Zaki repeated.

"Yes, tell us, Zaki, what came first the chicken or the egg?" Blake smiled.

"Well, according to some scientists, there was a Big Bang of matter, an expanding universe," Zaki began. "A mass of matter expanding created planets and the universe."

"And where did this matter come from, Zaki?" Blake asked.

"There is no satisfactory theory as to the appearance of this matter," Zaki answered. "There are theories about a universe collapsing and expanding to create the world we now know as the universe."

"But where did the matter come from?" Blake repeated.

"That is difficult to answer in a satisfactory manner," Zaki replied.

"There is no satisfactory answer because no one knows. Isn't that right, little man?"

"No, you don't understand about the different theories involved in answering such a question."

"Different theories, bah, Zaki Friedman. How will the world end?"

"There are many theories to answer such an inquiry," Zaki replied. "It may end in a Big Freeze or in intense heat. It all depends on how the Sun will die."

"But it is all theories, right, little man? No one knows the answer to such a question."

"We can theorize based on different models on the demise of stars."

"It is a question that can't be answered—"

"It can be answered utilizing different models—"

"No answer!" Blake shouted. "How about is the Bible true?"

"There are certain elements of the Bible that are almost certainly based on truths and events that occurred."

"Almost certainly?"

"That is all we can say at the present time—"

"No one knows for sure, right, little man?"

"There are certain events which we can prove utilizing ancient accounts by historians of the area—"

"Was there a flood?"

"There is some speculation that there will be remains found—"

"Was there a flood in China?"

"There is no evidence of a flood in China, although a satisfactory study—"

"Bah, there is no study and there is no answer," Blake roared. "Is there a God?"

"There is some question on exactly what would constitute a God of some kind and the location of such a Being."

"Is it a he or a she, Zaki? What does it look like?"

"There is some speculation that it might be androgynous in some way and may be located in another dimension."

"Yeah, right, another dimension. You don't know, do you, Zaki Friedman?"

Zaki shifted in his seat. He didn't know whether to stay on the set or just run away. He knew he would be attacked either way.

"You don't know the answer, little man!"

"Please, Mr. Warren," Megan was saying, trying to calm Blake down.

"How do you know the answers to all those questions? Do you have something on you that gives you the answers?"

Zaki stood up and pulled his pockets out. "I have nothing on me that performs such a function," he said.

"He cheats!" Blake was shouting. "He cheats!"

Zaki stood there as Blake dashed toward him. When he reached Zaki, Blake began pulling at his clothing.

"Please, Mr. Warren, we are on the air," Megan shouted.

Blake, meanwhile, was ripping Zaki's shirt. "Where is the device, Zaki?" Blake was screaming. "Where do you hide it?"

Just as he was about to rip Zaki's shirt off, a woman darted across the stage screaming. "No!" she shouted. "Let him be, Blake!"

Zaki looked to see Beth Miller attack Blake from behind. There was now total chaos on the stage.

"We will be back after these messages," Megan shouted, the light on the television camera blinking off. "What a great show," she said to her director.

"Stop it, Blake," Beth was saying, pulling at Blake's shirt. "Let him be, let him be."

Blake finally let go of Zaki's shirt and turned toward Beth. Zaki, meanwhile, ran from the stage and into the darkness.

They watched as Zaki crashed through the exit doors and vanished.

44

Zaki cried in the limousine all the way home. He would get even somehow, he told himself. When the limo reached the apartment building, he stumbled out the car door and ran to the doorman.

"Thank you, Charlie," he said, hurrying through the open front door.

He was soon standing inside the apartment, wondering how he was going to get even with Blake Warren.

"I hate that Blake Warren," he said to himself. "But I don't want to harm Beth Miller, she tried to help me."

He picked up one of the yellowing handkerchiefs on the floor of the apartment and sneezed into it. He then snorted and put the handkerchief in his pocket.

"What do I have that I can use on Blake Warren?" he asked himself. "One of the weapons I was developing—"

He walked to one of the rooms and opened a box that was lying on the floor. He then pulled out a long, black weapon.

"Yes, I was developing this one," he said to himself. "It should provide the necessary power needed."

He looked at the black weapon and smiled. "Yes, a disintegrator ray," he smiled. "Perfect for getting rid of that special someone."

He aimed it at the desk and pulled the trigger. Nothing happened. "All it needs are a few adjustments," he said, looking over the black weapon. "I don't think I have to go back to my laboratory to get it ready to use. No, it looks like just a few simple adjustments might do the trick."

Zaki began to laugh thinking about how he would use the disintegrator gun on Blake Warren. If the gun worked properly, there would be nothing left of Blake Warren except his underwear.

"I can do all the adjustments here," he said to himself. "Then I'll find Blake Warren."

He retrieved his tool box and started working on the gun. He used a screwdriver and some oil and the gun seemed to come alive in his chubby hands.

"There now, almost good to go," he smiled to himself. "There are going to be a lot of surprised faces when there's nothing but a spot left where Blake Warren is standing."

He then started to examine the severity dial on the top of the gun. "Well, let's see, should I keep him alive?" he asked himself. "Maybe just embarrass him might do the trick."

The dial marked either topical disintegration, medium disintegration, or total disintegration. It was now on topical disintegration.

"All I really want is the girl," he told himself. "Blake can have his useless little life if the girl cooperates."

He then took the gun to the window of the apartment and flipped the dial to total disintegration. "Let's just see what kind of power I do have," he mumbled to himself. "A little demonstration is definitely necessary."

He opened the window and listened to what was happening outside. He could see a cat walking along the sidewalk and decided that would be the gun's first test. Sticking the gun out the window, he aimed it at the cat.

"Ta ta, pussy willow," he muttered, holding the gun.

He then pulled the trigger. There was a flash of light and a sizzling beam and then the cat disappeared.

"Excellent," he told himself. "This thing works perfectly."

He pulled the gun inside and closed the window. "I'll take it to the studio and see if I can't have Blake summoned for another interview."

"This time, however, there will be no questions except one: Where is Blake Warren hiding?"

Zaki laughed and then he put the disintegrator gun in a bag. He then made a call to the studio asking whether another interview could be arranged with Blake Warren. Megan told him Blake was in the studio to do a follow-up interview. She told him to come to the studio and he would be very much welcomed.

Zaki left the apartment and made his way to the elevator. The hallway was empty as he carried the bag to the doors. This was going to be very simple. He would disintegrate Blake at a break or something when they were alone. Then he would tell everyone Blake excused himself and didn't say where he was going. Before anyone knew what was happening, he would be far away telling everyone he had no idea what had happened to Blake. It would be very simple.

As the doors of the elevator opened, some guy pushed past Zaki and hurried into the elevator. "I don't think you should have done that," he said to the man.

"Stick it, sonny," the man replied.

Zaki laughed and stepped into the elevator. When the doors closed, he pulled out the disintegrator gun. "Ever seen one of these?" he asked the man.

The man started to shake. "I didn't mean to upset you, sir," he pleaded.

'But you did upset me," Zaki replied.

"No, no, sir, please, I have children," the man said.

Zaki set the dial at topical disintegration and pulled the trigger. A blast of light came pouring out and then the man was standing there in his underwear, t-shirt and socks.

"Have a good day, sonny," Zaki said, putting the gun back in the shoulder bag. "If you tell anyone, I'll vaporize everybody."

The elevator doors opened, and Zaki walked across the lobby. He was soon back outside and heading for the limousine.

"We're going to the television studio," he told the driver. "We have to hurry."

Zaki sat down in the back and the limo slid out into the avenue. No one except for Blake would know about the gun, he told himself. All he needed was a few minutes alone with him.

There was a lot of traffic. Zaki wondered if he'd ever get to the studio. The limo slowly made its way down the street. Then all traffic halted. There was an accident or something and Zaki knew what he had to do.

Zaki got out of the limo carrying the shoulder bag. "I'll be right back after I solve this traffic jam," he told the driver.

The driver nodded, and Zaki made his way around the stationary cars. He kept walking until he spotted the cause of the traffic jam. Two cars had hit each other right near the intersection. If everyone waited for the authorities, the mess would probably be cleaned up in hours. Zaki didn't want to wait.

Taking the disintegrator gun out of the shoulder bag, he watched as people gasped or ran. Several people put their arms in the air pleading with

Zaki not to shoot them. He walked past them, still holding the gun, and stopped in front of the dented cars.

"Whose cars are these?" he asked.

One of the men looked annoyed. "You going to shoot everybody?" he growled, "because of a damned fender bender?"

"Yes, shoot this sucker," said the other man. "He rammed his car right into me for no reason at all."

"Oh, there was a reason," said the man. "You were too stupid to get out of the way. I was in a hurry, man."

They looked at Zaki, who was holding the gun and turning toward the two cars.

"You can't shoot it out of the way, sir," one of the men said. "They're coming to tow them right now."

"I have no time to waste waiting for them to come," Zaki replied. "I have to go somewhere."

Zaki then turned the severity dial on the gun to total disintegration. He pointed the gun at the two cars and pulled the trigger. There was a terrific blast of light, a sizzling beam, and then the cars were gone.

"What did you do with my car, man?" asked one of the men.

"It's somewhere where it can't block traffic," Zaki replied.

"But that was my car," moaned the other man.

"Sue me," Zaki said, walking back to the limo.

As he put the gun back in the shoulder bag, a teenager saw the huge, bulbous head and gasped. "Hey, you're that genius on TV," he shouted.

"Not now, kid," Zaki said, heading back to the limo.

"But you know the answer to everything," the boy said.

"I have to get going, sorry, kid."

Zaki got back into the limo and told the driver to hit the gas. The studio was only a few blocks away. Zaki was now ready for Blake and anyone else who got in his way. The gun had been successfully tested and now he was confident his plan would work.

When they reached the studio, Zaki got out of the limo holding the shoulder bag. He told the driver to wait for him and then he walked inside the building.

"Look who's here now," Megan greeted him as he stepped into the studio.

"Is Blake here?" he asked.

"He's getting ready in the back," Megan told him. "You want to go to makeup?"

Zaki shook his head. "No time, Megan," he said. "A little touch up will have to do."

Zaki was holding the shoulder bag when Blake Warren finally appeared on stage. "You've come back for more, little man?" he said with a laugh. "I thought you learned your lesson."

"Well, I figured it's your time to learn, Blake," he replied.

"Very witty, little man."

"Quiet, people," Megan said. "We're ready to go on the air."

"Well, you introduce Blake first and then I'll come on," Zaki told her.

"Better do as he says, Megan," Blake joked. "He just might beat everybody up if he doesn't get his way."

Everyone laughed and then the light on the television camera blinked on. "Hello, everybody, and welcome to our show," Megan began. "We have with us today two opposing forces. You remember them from our last show? Yes, that's right, Blake Warren and Zaki Friedman—"

Zaki was waiting for Megan to introduce Blake and then he would pull the disintegrator gun out of the bag.

"First of all, we have with us a director—"

Zaki slipped the gun out of the bag and made sure the dial was on medium disintegration. He then stepped forward and aimed it at Blake.

"What the hell is that?" Blake shouted as Zaki pulled the trigger.

There was a burst of light, a sizzling beam, and then Blake was enshrouded. In seconds, the light faded and so did Blake's clothing. Standing there on national television, Blake Warren was completely naked.

"Oh, my God!" screamed Megan, trying to get out of the way.

"You little worm!" shouted Blake, jumping behind the couch.

Zaki put the gun in the bag, and then walked toward the exit doors. He heard someone running toward him from behind.

"Zaki!" the female voice shouted.

He turned around and saw Beth standing there with a smile. "Great job, Zaki," she said, holding out her hand. "Take me with you."

"Yes, it would be my pleasure, Beth Miller."

They walked out the doors and headed for the limo.

"You're coming back to the apartment, Beth Miller?" he asked.

"Yes, Zaki, I've had enough of Blake Warren,"

"It's good to hear you say that."

They made their way to the limo and slid inside. "He was such a jerk," Beth said with a laugh.

"Who is that?" Zaki asked.

"Blake Warren," she said. "He was a creep and a jerk and I'll never see him again as long as I live."

"Did he hit you at all?" Zaki wondered.

She frowned. "I never should have left you, Zaki," she said. "You were right the whole time. I liked him because he was pretty. I'm never going to make that mistake again."

"Then you don't mind if I'm a monster, Beth Miller?"

"Oh, you're not a monster, Zaki. Don't even say it in jest."

"Then you still like me?"

"Of course, Zaki, I never stopped liking you."

"Do you want me to go back and disintegrate Blake?" he asked.

Beth laughed. "Did you see his face when you hit him with that ray?" she said. "I've never seen anyone so angry and confused. When did you invent that gun, Zaki? Was it just to use on Blake?"

"I wanted to get even somehow," he explained. "Especially since he had you, Beth dear."

"Well, you got even all right, Zaki. I mean I don't think we'll ever see Blake again after that embarrassing moment on television. I mean he was stark naked on national television, Zaki."

"It will probably be all over the internet, too," he said.

"Serves that jerk right."

"He had it coming to him."

"Oh, Zaki, you were outstanding."

"You really think so, Beth dear?"

"Yes, I mean you really took command of the situation and then let him have it just like he deserved."

"I didn't want to disintegrate him, though."

"You mean that thing actually can wipe a person off the planet, Zaki?"

He nodded his head. "It was one of my weapon ideas that I decided to finish for this occasion," he said with a smile.

"Pretty unbelievable. You'd better make sure no one gets their hands on it, Zaki. I mean somebody can do unbelievable damage with such a weapon."

"I think I'll destroy it, dear. I'll make sure no one else can use it for any kind of purpose."

"Yes, that would be the wise thing to do, Zaki."

The limo halted and they got out and walked to the door.

"Hey, it's that genius," somebody said. "He knows everything."

Zaki waved to everyone as they walked onward.

"Hey, what's the Penguin's real name?" somebody shouted.

"Oswald Chesterfield Cobblepot," Zaki replied.

"The guy's outrageous," some guy said.

"A real genius," agreed someone else.

Zaki, meanwhile, grabbed Beth's hand as they walked inside the apartment building, the crowd applauding behind them.

45

Welcome to today's second round of "Pop Quiz"—
Sen, please choose from today's categories—
The Human Body for $400—
What does Broca's area control?—
Zaki?
Speech—
Correct for $400—
Zaki's choice—
Who's Who for $400—
What was Sojourner Truth's real name?—
Zaki?
Isabella, she was a slave.
Correct for $400—
Okay, Zaki, it's your choice—
Animals for $400—
What mammal has the longest life span?—
Zaki—
Human beings—
Correct for $400—
Zaki—
American History for $400—
How long did the Pony Express last?—
Zaki?—
About 18 months—
That is correct for $400—
Zaki, it's once again your choice—
American History for $800—

Who founded Detroit?—

Zaki—

Antoine Cadillac—

Correct for $800, and of course, the automobile was named for him—

Zaki's choice—

The Human Body for $800—

How much is the human body worth?—

Zaki?—

About $170,000—

That is actually the correct answer, although some people think it is between 98 cents and $5—

Very good, Zaki, we'll be back after these important messages--

46

Zaki and Beth were married on a warm day in the spring. Everybody came, although not everyone was sure why Beth would marry him. After all, she was a pretty woman who could have her pick of the eligible men and he was Zaki, a genius to be sure, but still someone with a huge head and small body who needed a handkerchief much too much.

"Hi, Beth," greeted Jeremiah, wearing a pair of thick glasses.

"Why the glasses?" Zaki asked.

"Special glasses, Zaki dear, I had them made myself," he replied.

"Let me see those things, Jerry."

"Can't stay, my friend, and congratulations," Jeremiah said, walking away into the crowd.

"Can't stay, my foot," Zaki muttered, deciding to follow him.

When he caught up with him again, he reached for the glasses. "Let me see those things, Jerry," he said.

"Please, Zaki, they're only glasses so I can see," Jeremiah replied. "I don't think you have to mock me."

Just then, Beth's cousin, a beautiful woman with light blond hair, came strolling down the walkway. Zaki looked for a second and then was caught by the expression on Jeremiah's face – he was grinning from ear to ear.

Zaki slowly walked over and then pulled Jeremiah's glasses from his head. Jeremiah screamed for a moment, and then hurried after his older brother.

"So you need these glasses to see," Zaki said to him. "What the hell are you doing, Jerry, don't you think someone will become suspicious?"

"No one knows about the View Finder except you Zaki. I mean you invented the darned thing. I think it's the greatest invention in the history of mankind. But they're a bit bulky, Zaki, so I had a pair made that you can wear to parties and things and not be suspected of doing anything wrong."

"You can see everything with these things," Zaki grumbled, "even my bride."

"I try not to look at her, Zaki," Jeremiah explained. "I just wanted to see everyone else who was coming. Like those cousins of hers."

"Well, your days of looking at the cousins is over, Jerry."

"You're not taking the glasses, are you, Zaki?"

"Yes, I'm taking the glasses, Jerry, and I don't want to see you wearing another pair later in the day."

"Would I do that?"

Zaki put the View Finder glasses in his pocket and walked away. Jeremiah smiled, reached into his pocket and pulled out another pair of View Finder glasses.

"Should be a really good party," he said to himself, smiling.

Zaki, meanwhile, walked back to where Beth was standing. "Hello, dear," he said, putting Jeremiah's glasses into his front pocket. "What did I miss?"

"What did you just put in your pocket, Zaki?" she asked.

"Oh, nothing, Jeremiah had a pair of prank glasses."

"Prank glasses?"

"Yeah, they weren't real or anything."

"I just may want to wear them, Zaki."

"They're not real, Beth, you would only look weird."

"Is that what you think?"

He didn't have a chance to reply. Before he knew it, she pulled the glasses from his pocket and swung them in the air.

"So you think I would look weird, huh, Zaki?"

"Really, Beth, you have no time to fool around with party glasses."

"Yes, I do."

She put the glasses on her face and then halted. She looked at Zaki and screamed.

"You don't understand, Beth, they weren't meant to be used by anyone."

"Yeah, right, then how did Jeremiah get them?"

"All right, I invented them but they weren't meant to be used as glasses."

"Oh, my God, Zaki, you can see everything with these things."

"Yes, Beth, but they were going to be destroyed—"

"Destroyed? But you gave them to Jeremiah."

"But he had them made into glasses, dear."

"Don't you dear me, Zaki, these things can see everything."

He was still pleading his case when she gave the glasses to one of her cousins. The cousin put the glasses on and began to scream in high-pitched shrieks.

"Oh, my God," the cousin screamed, running to her car.

"Do you see what you've done, Zaki?"

"But they were meant for lonely guys on a Saturday night, Beth dear."

"Yeah, right."

Beth's father, Arnold Miller, came running to his daughter after hearing the argument. "You kids are fighting already?" he said, putting his arms around his angry daughter.

"Zaki has invented something," she explained.

"Another new invention?" her father said. "What's wrong with that?"

"Well, you haven't seen the invention."

"What's wrong with it, Beth?"

"Well, it can see things," she explained.

"See things? What kind of things?"

Beth held the glasses up in her hand. "Well, Zaki, should I let Daddy have a look at the invention?"

Zaki frowned. "I don't think that's a really good idea, Beth dear," he said.

"Why not?" she asked with a laugh, "just because it can see things that other people can't see with their eyes?"

"I think I must doze for a moment," Zaki muttered. "I really must relax and ease the stress in my life."

"Oh, Zaki, don't you want to stay up and see what you've been missing?" Beth shouted so that everyone could hear.

"Let me see those glasses," her father interrupted.

"Oh, you'll get a real kick out of them, father," Beth said.

Beth's father grabbed the glasses and put them on his face. In a moment, they were back off in his hand.

"That's what you invented? Dirty glasses? After you marry my daughter? Are you sick in the head, you over-educated moron?"

"No, you don't understand, Mr. Miller," Zaki pleaded. "They weren't meant to be used by anyone. I was going to have them destroyed."

"Someone should have you destroyed!" shouted Beth's father.

"What's going on here?" Zaki's father, Marvin, wanted to know.

"Do you see these filthy things that your very sick son invented?"

Beth's father handed Marvin Friedman the glasses. He put them on his face and then started shouting.

"You lunatic, Zaki, what the hell have you done?" he screamed.

"But they were for young guys out for a good time," Zaki explained. "No one was supposed to get hurt—"

"Get hurt?" Marvin Friedman repeated. "You want everyone to see what everyone looks like in their birthday suits? Are you nuts or something?"

"But Jeremiah had them made into glasses—"

"Your brother had something to do with this?"

"No, I can explain, Pop," Jeremiah interrupted. "These are trick glasses. You're really not seeing what you think you're seeing, the glasses are only tricking you into thinking you're seeing what you think you're seeing."

"What are trying to say, son?" asked Marvin Friedman.

"That it's all one big illusion, Pop," Jeremiah explained with a smile. "You can't really see what your brain is telling you what you're seeing. Isn't that right, Zaki?"

Zaki paused for a moment, and then realized what he had to do. "Oh, yes, father," he finally said. "I put a screen inside the glasses so it only seems as if you're seeing what you think you're seeing. In reality, you're only seeing what I want you to see and not what you think you're seeing."

"So we only think we're seeing what we're seeing," his father said.

"That's right, father. It would be illegal to allow anyone to see what everyone thinks everyone is seeing, so therefore there's something in the glasses that makes you think you're seeing what it would be illegal to see."

"Well, there's your explanation," his father said to Beth's father. "You're not really seeing what you really think you're seeing."

"Well, I see what I see and these glasses are not going to be seen again," Beth's father replied. "I'm putting these things where nobody can see anything whether they want to or not. How do you like that?"

"Do what you must do," Jeremiah said. "Nobody was using them, anyway."

"And nobody will ever use them again," Beth's father growled.

He then carried the glasses to a nearby wall and began smashing them to pieces. When all that was left was the frame, he handed it back to Zaki.

"Don't let me catch you wearing these things again," he warned.

"Nobody saw anything," Zaki said. "Not anything they thought they saw, anyway."

Jeremiah walked away smiling. When he disappeared around a corner, he reached into his pocket for another pair of the glasses. "I really want to see what I'm not supposed to be seeing," he said to himself with a laugh.

Jeremiah watched the whole wedding ceremony with a huge smile on his face. It was the most enjoyable affair he had ever been to, although he wouldn't tell Zaki or anyone else.

47

Welcome to the Final Quiz question—

The contestants will have thirty seconds to write down their answers to the Final Quiz question. But first, they must make a wager—

The wagers are now in and we're ready for today's Final question—

Here it is—

What is an erythrophobe?—

Contestants, you have thirty seconds—

Fifteen—

Ten—

Okay, let's look at what our contestants wrote down—

Let's start with Kiara—

She wrote down, "fear of lightning."—

Incorrect, how much did you wager? All of it, I'm very sorry—

Let's now go to Dennis—

What did he write down?—

"Fear of music"—

Incorrect. How much did you wager? Everything except one dollar—

All right, it's up to Zaki Friedman—

Zaki, did you get the right answer?—

"Someone who blushes easily"—

That is correct. Unbelievable, Zaki, you've done it again—

How much will he take home?—

$53,000 for a grand total of nine million nine hundred and fifty thousand dollars—

Incredible, Zaki, although I understand you're going to make an important statement tonight—

"That's right, Johnny. I feel I've won enough on 'Pop Quiz,' so I'm going to resign from the show at almost the ten million dollar mark."

Applause from the audience—

Well, I'm sure you thought long and hard about this decision, Zaki—

"Oh, yes, but I thought it was time to leave."

What will you remember most?—

"I'll remember how nice everybody has been to me, but so much has happened in my life since I first appeared on this program."

Yes, Zaki is now married everyone and he and his wife will enjoy all the money that Zaki has earned—

"Yes, that's right, Johnny, we can really live a nice life."

Well, let's hear it for our retiring champion, Zaki Friedman—

Applause from the audience—

Probably the best contestant to ever appear on a game show—

Thanks, everybody, we'll have three new contestants next time so join us for "Pop Quiz." Until then, good-bye everybody!

48

Zaki and Beth moved to a huge mansion in the suburbs with the money from the game show, his inventions, and commercials. Together, the couple had millions of dollars to begin a family and live happily ever after. One day, Beth informed Zaki of some very good news in the Friedman household.

"I'm going to have a baby," she told him. "I'm pregnant."

"How did that happen?" Zaki asked.

"Oh, there are ways," she replied. "What do you think we were doing together, Zaki dear?"

"Well, of all things, Beth dear, I didn't expect another mouth to feed."

"Zaki."

He smiled. "I'm only kidding, my dear, I think it's wonderful news. I'll get started on a computerized walking device right away. That way the baby can walk around the house at a very young age."

"I'm so happy, Zaki."

"Yes, we've been very lucky, my dear."

As the months sped by, Zaki worked on the computerized walker. He also invented a computerized spoon that showed the temperature of a solution and what it was made of. He was really happy about having a baby with Beth. It was the best thing to ever have happened to him. He still couldn't believe that Beth was going to be the mother of the child. His child.

"Zaki, I think it's time," Beth said to him one night as they were getting ready for bed.

"Time for what, Beth dear?"

"Time for the baby, Zaki."

"Baby?"

"Yes, you know, the baby that's inside me right now—"

"Well, what about it?"

"It wants to come out, Zaki dear."

"Oh, the baby, the baby," Zaki began to nervously mutter.

"Get my bag, Zaki, and then alert the driver that we will be going to the hospital tonight."

"Baby? Driver? Hospital? I think I must doze for a moment."

"Zaki, I need to go to the hospital, dear, there's no time to sleep right now."

"Right. Hospital."

Zaki grabbed one of the suitcases near the bed and fell to the floor.

"That was so light," he groaned, lying on the floor.

"There was nothing in that one, Zaki," Beth said. "The other one is the one I'm taking to the hospital."

"Hospital!"

"Just take your time, dear, and everything will be all right."

"Hospital!" Zaki shouted once again, getting off the floor. He subsequently tripped over the suitcase and fell to the floor again.

"Zaki, if you don't get off the floor, we'll never get there," Beth said, trying to stay calm.

"I think I hurt my back, Beth dear. I don't know if I can get up."

Beth waddled to the door and began shouting to one of the helpers. "Please I need to get to the hospital," she said.

They carried Beth and Zaki to the limo and then one of the servants brought the suitcases down and they sped off to the hospital. The baby, a girl, was born a few hours later.

"My daughter was born on Women's Equality Day, August 26," Zaki said to one of the nurses. "She will be a great female scientist or leader, her birthday being the birthdays of Mother Teresa; vice-presidential candidate Geraldine Ferraro; scientist Antoine-Laurent Lavoisier, the father of modern chemistry, and Albert Sabin, who developed the polio vaccine. On her birthday in 1920, the Nineteenth Amendment, granting women the right to vote, took effect. Yes, a great birthday, indeed, and because she will be brilliant everyone will say that she is 'one smart cookie,' which is why we'll call her, Cookie. Yes, Cookie Friedman, the smartest female to ever live on the planet!"

When he told Beth, she smiled and agreed. "Yes, Cookie is a good name for her, Zaki," she said. "It has a good-natured feel to it, something

I hope my daughter can live up to. Oh, Zaki, let's hope she is the smartest female ever."

"Well, I have been wiring the house for her, Beth dear," Zaki explained. "I'll help her in whatever ways I can."

"Let's make sure she has all the inspiration we can give her, Zaki," she replied. "I want only the best for her."

"With you as her mother, she already has the best," Zaki said. "But I'll do what I can to keep her little brain sharp."

Zaki then went home and made sure the whole house was wired as he had planned. At the time he had started the wiring, he didn't care whether it was a boy or a girl. But now that he knew it was a girl, it made him happy to finish the new sound system.

When Beth came home with little Cookie, Zaki had the house ready for their arrival. "News from Verona!" blared through the many speakers set up throughout the house. "How now, Balthasar!"

"What is that?" Beth wanted to know.

"I've wired the house and set up a sound system for Cookie," Zaki explained. "Now wherever she may be, Shakespeare will be playing through the speakers and soothing her young brain."

"Only Shakespeare?" Beth asked.

"Not only Shakespeare, my love, but Beethoven, Bach, and Mozart, too," he answered. "We will have the greatest music ever written playing through our house as well. But it doesn't stop there, Beth. I've arranged for subjects such as Physics and Calculus to be broadcast through the house. No matter where little Cookie goes, there will be stimulation for her developing brain and soul."

Beth smiled and then fell asleep. Zaki could see that she was happy with his plan to keep Cookie sharp and alert.

He made his way to little Cookie's room, and watched her lying there with her eyes closed in utter contentment. "The world will be yours, my little dear," he told her. "You will be everything everybody ever wanted in a female. You will be rich and powerful and the smartest person who ever lived."

Cookie smiled. He had already set up a system that if she cried or was upset or wanted anything, he could hear her throughout the house, her voice gaining precedence over the music and the Shakespeare readings.

"And if you can communicate in any way, my little dear, the Magic Board will help relay your words," he told his little daughter.

The Magic Board was a screen on which words could be typed or written to communicate with somebody else. It even had a microphone for voice communication. The voice was transcribed as words on the screen.

"The minute she can communicate, I will know about it," Zaki said. "There will be no doubt about her intelligence and her capacity for learning."

He stood there and looked at his new daughter. She was quite pretty, he thought to himself, with two big chocolate brown eyes and a cute smile. He wanted her to be everything he hoped she would be -- the greatest female genius in the history of the world.

Zaki remembered he had added something to the Humma. Now no matter what someone uttered into the microphone, a voice would mimic the words. If one wanted to he or she could convert the sounds into music.

Zaki brought the Humma into Cookie's room and put the microphone in front of her mouth. Cookie made all kinds of sounds with her lips and mouth which only the Humma could interpret into real sentences of some kind.

"Are you happy, my little darling?" Zaki asked her.

Cookie made sounds with her tiny lips. "I am quite content," the Humma machine interpreted. "Very happy."

Zaki smiled. Yes, it was possible to communicate with the very young, although it was doubtful they had much to say at such a young age.

"You want to sleep, young darling?" Zaki asked.

Cookie answered again in seeming gibberish. "Yes, must doze," the Humma machine interpreted. "Must sleep."

Zaki laughed. "She is definitely my daughter," he said. "I'll be interested to see how she develops in the coming months."

He looked down. There was something written on the Magic Board. "I love you," the message said.

Zaki looked at the message and sighed. "She is quite unbelievable already," he said. "She can already communicate and that is quite fascinating."

When Cookie finally fell asleep, he went upstairs to tell Beth what had happened. She was quite surprised when she heard the news and delighted that her young daughter could communicate in some way.

"Oh, Zaki, do you think she'll be everything we want her to be?" Beth asked.

"There's a good chance, Beth dear," Zaki replied. "Her eyes are quite bright and she seems to be somewhat aware of her surroundings."

"Oh, I only hope she proves to be something special, Zaki," she said. "I was really hoping she would be."

Zaki seemed to understand now why Beth loved him so. She seemed to feel Zaki could help her produce something special in the world. This child of theirs was going to be a shining light of some kind and Beth was content that she had something to do with it.

"You will be one proud mother, Beth dear," he finally said to her. "You gave her all the best and she will use it in the coming years."

"I sure hope so, Zaki,' she replied. "She was unusually large for a female baby. I think that's a good sign. She will be tough and powerful, something males will have to acknowledge in some way."

"In the beginning God created the heaven and the earth." The words echoed through the house in a deep male voice.

"And what's that, Zaki?" Beth wondered. "It sounds like the Bible."

"It is the Bible, dear," he said. "I thought the Bible should also be a part of little Cookie's education."

"It sounds like the voice of God," Beth said. "I think it's a good idea for little Cookie to hear the words."

"Then she can decide for herself."

"Decide what, Zaki?"

"Decide if she believes in those words. I think I'll play someone reading from Darwin next. Little Cookie will be exposed to all points of view."

"Yes, good idea, Zaki. Then she can decide what the truth really is."

"And God said, Let there be light: and there was light."

The words reverberated through the house.

"She must think she's in heaven or something," Zaki laughed. "It truly is like hearing the voice of God Himself."

"Well, at least the words are soothing," Beth said. "I hope she enjoys them."

"I'll go see for myself, Beth dear. I'll tell you what her reaction was."

Zaki walked to Cookie's room and peered inside.

"And God said, Let there be a firmament in the midst of the waters, and let it divide the waters from the waters."

The words sailed through the calm air.

He glanced at his little daughter lying in the crib and smiled. She was lying on her back laughing, her big chocolate brown eyes sparkling in the light.

"You like God, darling?" he asked, placing the Humma microphone underneath her lips.

"God good," she said, her lips making all kinds of noises.

"Yes, my dear, God good," Zaki repeated. "Maybe she'll turn out to be a religious figure of some kind."

"And God said, Let the waters under the heaven be gathered together unto one place, and let the dry land appear: and it was so."

The words wafted through the calm air, causing little Cookie to giggle. Zaki wondered why the words would cause her to giggle.

"I hope that's not criticism," he said to her. "That might just get you in a lot of hot water, young lady."

Cookie kept giggling.

"What's so funny, my dear?" Zaki asked.

Cookie didn't answer.

"But it's God's words, my little lady."

He looked down at the Magic Board. There were words appearing on the screen as Cookie giggled once again.

"God good," the words said.

49

Cookie started talking at two months old. Shakespeare had been playing through the house, and when Beth went to pick her up, little Cookie said, "Bard."

"Bard?" Beth repeated.

Cookie smiled. "Bard," she said once again.

"Zaki, will you come here," she shouted. "Cookie is talking."

Her words were broadcast through the house via Zaki's sound system.

"Her first words, Zaki, and they were about Shakespeare," she told Zaki, who had appeared at the doorway. "What do you think of that?"

"I think it's wonderful, Beth dear," he said.

"But about Shakespeare and not her own mother or father?"

"That's the price we must pay for educating the very smart," Zaki replied. "You see, mother or father would have been too mundane for our little daughter, Beth dear. No, for a genius, mother or father is just too common. For her, appealing to the Bard was the only thing she could do."

"Okay, Zaki, but I still would have preferred Mommy or Daddy."

"Mommy or Daddy, bosh," Zaki said. "She wants to be great, my dear."

They looked at Cookie, who was smiling.

"Mama," she finally said.

Beth smiled. "Common or not, now I'm happy, Zaki dear," she said.

"But I'm not," he replied.

"Oh, don't worry she'll be saying Daddy before too long. Remember, dear, she wants to be great."

"What the heck is that supposed to mean?" Zaki asked.

"Well, you said it yourself, Zaki dear. She doesn't want to say the common words like Daddy or Papa."

Zaki walked over to Cookie, who was now sitting in the computerized walker, and smiled at her. "Daddy?" he said.

"Mama," was the reply.

"It's a conspiracy," Zaki complained. "I knew it as soon as I found out she was a female. A blasted conspiracy."

"Who's conspiring against you, Zaki?" Beth wanted to know.

"You are," he replied. "The females of this house are conspiring against me."

"Oh, come on, Zaki, she's two months old."

"Oh, but it's there, it's in the genes," Zaki said. "Females conspiring against the male population."

"Really, Zaki."

"Oh, don't tell me you don't know about it, Beth dear. I see it all the time out there. Females conspiring against men."

"It's only your imagination, Zaki dear."

"My imagination? Watch this—"

He smiled at Cookie once again. "Da-ddy," he said.

"Mama," Cookie replied.

"You see? My own daughter conspiring against me."

"She doesn't even know what you're talking about, Zaki."

"But you do, Beth, and you spend more time with her than anyone else."

"So now I taught her not to say Daddy, is that it?"

"Bingo. Female conspiracy."

"I think you've gone nuts, Zaki."

"Conspiracy."

"Bananas, that's it. You've gone bonkers just when your little daughter needs you most of all."

"She needs me? You really think so?"

"Yes, look at her. She wants her Daddy's love."

Zaki smiled. "Is that true, my little angel?" he asked. "You need your Daddy?"

"Mama," Cookie replied.

"That's it, conspiracy!"

Beth laughed.

"What's so funny, Beth dear?"

"You, thinking there's some kind of conspiracy."

"But females are like that, Beth dear, always figuring out ways to drive the male of the species totally crazy."

"And apparently succeeding."

"Yes, laugh now, but males will get their revenge."

"Revenge? They've been oppressing females since the beginning of time, Zaki dear. Any revenge will be taken by females."

"There! You admitted it: females are trying to get their revenge."

"Oh, come on, Zaki, the only thing females want is to be treated like any other human being."

"I still say there's a conspiracy."

"Oh, Zaki, enough of this nonsense—"

"Dada," Cookie suddenly said.

"She said it! My daughter said Dada!"

"What about the female conspiracy, Zaki?" Beth asked.

"Female conspiracy? I don't know what you're talking about. Is there something going on behind my back?"

"Oh, Zaki, you are a fruitcake."

"But a genius nonetheless."

"Yes, a genius, Zaki."

"Aha! There is some sort of female conspiracy!"

"Dada," Cookie said.

"Don't say his name, Cookie darling, there's something seriously wrong with your Dada. He has this crazy idea that we are in cahoots."

"Mama," Cookie replied.

"There it is, evidence that you two are working against me."

"You see, Cookie darling? Your Dada is quite crackers."

"Oh, you always know what to say my dear. Thanks a lot."

"It's your own fault, Zaki. You're the one who started on this whole female conspiracy thing."

"And there's not?"

"There will be now."

"What do you mean, Beth dear?"

"I plan to start one right away. Now take your daughter for a walk and try to make peace."

Zaki nodded and walked beside his young daughter as she shuffled along inside the computerized walker. It was like a doughnut with little Cookie moving her legs in the center. The walker was programmed to keep a certain path although it allowed the child to stray somewhat.

"What's this?" Cookie suddenly asked, pointing at the walker.

"Gosh, I thought I was done with questions," Zaki muttered, shaking his head. "That, darling, is the walker, your own computerized walker."

"What does it do?" Cookie asked.

"It gets you from one point to another, my little angel."

"What's this?"

"That is your computerized bottle, my darling. It tells you what liquid is inside, its temperature, how much is left, and when it was last used. A very good idea, wouldn't you say?"

"Very good," Cookie agreed.

"Yes, that was Dada's idea, my little wonder. I thought of it just for you, darling."

"Me have idea," Cookie said.

"I have an idea," Zaki corrected. "What is the idea, my little sugar bear?"

"Thingy thing."

Zaki smiled. "You must be a little more specific than that, my little darling," he said. "What kind of thingy thing?"

"Thing to play with."

"Yes, my sugar baby, a thingy thing to play with. What kind of things does the thingy thing have?"

"Things to use, round things and square things."

"It sounds like a terrific thing, my sweetheart, except I need a little more information before I can start designing such a thing."

"Things to use."

"I know what we'll do, my little flower. We'll get the Thinking Cap and it will tell me what you're thinking."

"Yes, good," little Cookie said with a smile.

"It sounds like an extraordinary new invention, my darling. I'm interested to hear all about it, but without the Thinking Cap I fear that would take years."

"Thingy thing."

"Yes, I know, dear, a thingy thing with round and square shapes."

They walked to Zaki's laboratory in the back of the house where Zaki retrieved the Thinking Cap. He placed the computerized cap on her head and tightened the strap. The Thinking Cap immediately began to buzz and beep.

"Thingy thing," Cookie mumbled as the lights flashed on and off.

"What exactly is a thingy thing?" Zaki asked.

"Gadget board for little ones," Cookie suddenly explained as the Thinking Cap began to blink.

"Gadget board? What a good idea, little one."

"Yes, little ones will like it," Cookie said as the Thinking Cap interpreted her thoughts.

"With round and square shapes?"

"Yes, things for concentration and inventiveness," Cookie said, the lights blinking and flashing.

"I understand," Zaki replied. "A gadget board with lots of little things to keep a young brain occupied. Yes, that is a good idea, my little darling."

Zaki bent down and unstrapped the Thinking Cap. He removed it from Cookie's head and placed it on a table.

"Thingy thing," Cookie said with a smile.

"Yes, of course, my little flower, a thingy thing to help all the young children think and dream."

"Yes, thingy thing."

50

"We're here with everybody's genius and answer man extraordinaire Zaki Friedman and his little daughter, Cookie, who may become the smartest female ever."

"What do you think about that, Cookie?"

"I think it's quite nice to be here," Cookie replied.

"Isn't that amazing, ladies and gentlemen? This little girl is not quite six-months-old and she's talking fluently and walking, too."

"Yes, Cookie is quite advanced for a child her age," Zaki said.

"Do you think she'll be as smart as you, Zaki?"

Zaki nodded. "It's quite possible, Chrissy," he said. "Cookie was reading almost as soon as she was born with the help of the Magic Board and the Humma."

"Both of those items were invented by you, Zaki, isn't that right?"

"Yes, I invented them, but I have made them available to the public."

"Didn't Cookie help you invent something for infants and children?"

Zaki nodded again. "Yes, she did, Chrissy," he said. "The computerized Gadget Board was Cookie's idea which I just refined to make it easier to use. But it was all Cookie's idea at about two months old."

"Unbelievable, ladies and gentlemen—"

Thunderous applause swept through the studio.

"And Cookie, how did you think of the Gadget Board?"

"I wanted to help little children achieve consciousness," Cookie explained.

"Wow, Cookie, you are pretty smart for a little child. How did you learn so much in such a short amount of time?"

"Mommy and Daddy helped me to read. They are very smart themselves and with the help of Daddy's inventions, I am able to think quite well."

"Daddy has a lot of inventions, doesn't he, Cookie?"

Cookie smiled into the television camera. "Oh, yes, he has invented so many things and I want to be just like him."

There was more applause from the audience.

"It sounds like you're almost like him already, dear."

There was more applause and laughter from the audience as Cookie smiled once again.

"Do you have some invention ideas, Cookie?"

"I would like to build a roller coaster across the United States," she said with a smile. "It would put many people to work and it would be fun to travel."

"Great, Cookie. Isn't she a little darling, folks?"

Everybody applauded as Cookie giggled for the crowd.

"She just might be right," Zaki interrupted. "I think a roller coaster would be a great idea. Maybe we should make all of the crumbling cities amusement parks. That would bring money in and provide jobs."

"I hear you two completed something very recently, what was it?"

"Animation Board," Cookie giggled. "I made it with Daddy."

"Yes, it's a simple enough invention, Chrissy," Zaki said. "It's a computerized board that allows one to draw on it and then animates whatever the person wants, creating their own cartoon. Children will have hours of fun creating their own cartoon shows."

"And this was Cookie's idea?"

Cookie smiled into the camera. "I was thinking what would children want to do to occupy their time."

"It's something useful and also takes time," Zaki added. "It's perfect for a long car ride or something to do instead of watching TV. Children can actually make their own animated TV shows with this."

"That's fabulous, Cookie. You are Daddy's little genius, aren't you?"

"I like being like my father very much," Cookie said with another smile.

"And I like you being like me," Zaki said.

"Well, now that everybody likes each other, I have another question. And speaking of questions, we hear Cookie can answer questions just like Daddy. Isn't that right?"

"Yes, but you have to be a little careful, Chrissy," Zaki explained. "She's a little young to answer anything. You can, however, ask her anything in certain categories. For instance, she knows Shakespeare and the Bible very well."

"Okay, Cookie, we'll start with the Bible. What are the names of the Four Horsemen of the Apocalypse?"

Cookie sat there in the television lights and laughed. "It's the Book of Revelation," she finally said. "The names were Conquest, Slaughter, Famine and Death."

"Very good, dear. Are you going to go on 'Pop Quiz,' too?"

"Not right now," Cookie replied.

"She's a little too young right now, Chrissy," Zaki said. "But she is learning everything she needs to know to eventually go on that show."

"And what about you, Zaki? How are you doing after retiring as undefeated champion from that show?"

"I'm doing quite fine. The money I won will be used for Cookie's education."

"And where do you suppose will she be going? Harvard, anyone?"

"I don't want to start her too early, though," Zaki replied.

"She already knows quite a lot just by you and your wife teaching her. Isn't that right, Zaki?"

"Well, the sound system and the Magic Board also helped a lot."

"What if we ask questions to father and daughter? How about that, ladies and gentlemen?"

"Okay, but Cookie prefers Shakespeare."

"We'll ask you both a Shakespeare question. First, for Cookie. What was Shakespeare's first play?"

"That would be *Henry VI, Part One*."

"And how old was he when he wrote it, Zaki?"

"About 25."

"Well, both father and daughter are absolutely correct."

"Yes, that was fun," Cookie laughed.

"They may be the smartest male and female in the world, ladies and gentlemen. And Cookie is not even a year old—"

"I'll come back when I'm one," Cookie said with a smile.

"What will she know by that time? It boggles the mind to think about it."

"Well, Cookie is going to start to think about what she wants to do in life," Zaki said.

"And what will that be, Zaki?"

"I don't know, maybe a doctor or a lawyer, but she will have to decide."

"But she's still so young."

"Yes, but it helps if one knows what one wants to do in life, Chrissy."

"Most children her age can't even speak or walk yet, Zaki. Aren't you afraid of pushing her too much?"

"No, I think Cookie will figure it out for herself. I have a lot of confidence in her and her developing brain."

"Well, Cookie, have you thought about what you would like to be?"

Cookie looked into the television camera and smiled. "I would like to be a doctor or scientist," she said. "Maybe invent things like my Daddy."

"Yes, she has already invented things with her Daddy, Chrissy," Zaki said. "There's really no telling what this little girl is capable of."

"And she already knows the answer to so many things, folks. How about another question having to do with the Bible, Cookie?"

"Yes, very good."

"What are the two specific animals on Noah's ark mentioned in the Bible?"

"Only two animals?"

"That's right, Cookie, only two animals are specifically mentioned—"

"They are birds, right, Daddy?"

"Yes, precious, they are birds."

"Then the answer is a raven and a dove."

"Yes, the birds sent out to see if the waters had dried. Very good, Cookie, you are almost as smart as your father already. And that's saying something, my friends, if you know anything about Zaki Friedman."

"I take it as a compliment, Chrissy," Zaki laughed. "Let's hope she's everything we all hope her to be."

"Zaki Friedman and his brilliant daughter, Cookie, who is only six months old, ladies and gentlemen—"

"Almost six months old," Zaki corrected.

"Almost six months, everybody. What do you think of them? We'll be back after these messages—"

51

Zaki was unhappy with the world. As much as he tried to keep a positive outlook on things, circumstances and human nature just kept getting in the way. Most people, he thought, didn't operate on much logic and were quick to fight with others about religion, ideology, love and money. There was a mass lunacy in the world and he was worried about what that meant for Cookie and her future. He decided he would do something about it.

He worked in his laboratory for weeks trying to solve the problems he had identified while living in the world. He decided he would take a positive approach in trying to solve those problems. He would invent a positive weapon to be used on differing human beings. Most weapons were negative in nature, essentially obliterating the enemy or opposition. This weapon would soothe the enemy or opposition and bring about some form of peace.

"The Positor," he announced to himself, "will not kill or maim another human being in any way." This would be the beginning of positive weapons, which were not meant to destroy but to heal. He decided he would use such a weapon to bring peace, not war, to this troubled world.

After months of work, he was finally ready to test his new invention – the greatest positive invention in history.

He sauntered down the street looking for someone on which he could test his new invention. He watched as two people were almost involved in an accident with their automobiles, and decided this is where he would first test the Positor.

"Why don't you look where you're going, you idiot," shouted one of the drivers, a middle-aged man with a bad temper.

"I would if you knew anything about driving," said the other, a younger man who seemed to want a physical fight.

The two men were getting out of their cars to settle the matter with their fists when Zaki let them have it. A brilliant ray flashed from the Positor and enveloped the two angry men. The ray seemed to sparkle and spin. Suddenly, the two men were smiling.

"How about downing a few beers?" one of them asked.

"Yes, it's time we got to know each other, my friend," the other said.

Zaki watched and smiled. The Positor was just the invention he was looking for, he said to himself. By using the gun, he could rid the world of animosity and bring peace and harmony to the world.

He placed the Positor in his shoulder bag and walked back to his home to tell Beth all about it. He wanted to get her reaction to the new invention and maybe listen to her suggestions on just how to use it correctly.

"The Positor?" she said upon hearing Zaki explain it for the first time. "And this gun can bring peace to the world?"

Zaki nodded. "This is the invention the world has been waiting for, Beth dear," he said. "I can end all arguments and disputes with one flick of a finger."

"Yes, very good, Daddy," Cookie said, as she sat there with her mother.

"Maybe you should end all warfare, Zaki dear," Beth said. "I mean if this weapon can be used for peace and not for war, well, it's about time, I say."

"Well, I've only been able to capture the ray in a gun," he told her. "I want to unleash the ray on the whole world in time."

"That's what the world needs, Zaki, a chance to know how peace really feels. It might be good to aim the ray at the entire world."

"Yes, Daddy could make hate go away," Cookie said.

"Let me try it out on you, Beth dear. I want to know if it's as effective as I think it is."

"Can it harm me at all, Zaki?"

"I don't think so. It's just a ray I developed from positively charged particles. I don't think it does any lasting damage to the people involved."

"Well, you better be sure, dear."

"You don't want even a little sample?"

"Not if it's going to hurt me, Zaki. Try it out on strangers if you must."

"I think I might just try it out on the leaders of the world," he replied. "I won't stop trying until there is complete peace in the world."

"Yes, I like the cause, Zaki dear, but I do hope you don't cause any harm."

"No, I'll make sure nothing is harmed, darling."

"We live near a big city, Zaki, I'm sure you can find a lot of disagreeable people to try the ray on."

"Yes, and before too long, everyone's negative thoughts will be converted to positive ones."

"It's worth trying, dear," she said.

Zaki knew right away where he wanted to test the gun. He placed it in his shoulder bag and then slid into the limousine.

"To the United Nations," he announced to the driver.

Zaki sat back and smiled. This was the perfect place to see if the gun would work on large crowds of people. It would also reveal whether the ray was effective against all peoples of the world.

When they reached Manhattan, Zaki wondered whether he would be allowed inside the General Assembly. They checked for weapons these days because of all the terrorism incidents. This was reversed terrorism, Zaki thought. This was going to be something new in the world. A radical peacenik who would stop at nothing to bring harmony to the world.

The limo suddenly pulled up in front of the United Nations building in midtown Manhattan. "You stay here and wait," he told the driver, "and I will be out in a few minutes."

He hoped no one would be chasing him out of the UN building. Not with the Positor ray, he told himself. And then Zaki realized as long as he had the gun in his hand, no one would complain about anything. That was it. He laughed to himself. Now he would really see if the Positor gun was ready for the world.

Taking the black gun out of the shoulder bag, Zaki stepped out of the limousine. The moment he was out of the limo, he heard shouting.

"Hey, that guy has a gun!" somebody screamed.

Zaki turned and fired the Positor at the man who was shouting. The dazzling ray sparkled in the sunshine. The man bathed in the ray for a few moments and then was suddenly smiling.

"Oh, what a silly person am I," the man now said. "He must be just playing around. Yes, playing, what a good idea."

"So far it works pretty well," Zaki said to himself. "These people become pretty happy after being hit by the ray."

He kept walking, firing the ray at anybody he saw near the entrance of the building. The ray sparkled and spun and then they seemed to be uncontrollably happy.

"Oh, what a beautiful day it is," one of the people exposed to the ray was saying. "It's a good thing I brought my happy face with me today."

Zaki smiled and continued walking to the UN entrance. He swung the door open and immediately opened fire with the Positor ray.

"Come right in, jolly sir," said someone at the door. "We didn't think you were a danger to anyone, we just wanted to play with our guns, too."

"Yes, but your guns can hurt someone," Zaki replied. "I suggest you put them away immediately."

"Yes, you are so right, smart gentleman," one of the security guards said with a smile. "Come right in and make yourself at home."

Zaki nodded. He turned and kept firing the Positor ray at anyone who seemed to be threatened by his presence. After a few moments, everyone seemed to be smiling.

"I am quite content," one woman said, who initially appeared to be quite frightened. "I didn't realize this young man was spreading good will to everyone. He is really a very nice gentleman."

Zaki stepped forward and opened the doors of the General Assembly. All of the world's representatives sat there in silence as Zaki entered.

"What do you want from us?" the Russian representative wanted to know. "Who are you and why do you want to spread terrorism?"

"I just want you to sit there and be nice," Zaki replied. "This is reversed terrorism, my friend. Everyone will soon be very nice to each other."

"Horrible," some of the other representatives shouted. "He is some sort of radical or something."

"Yes, maybe so," Zaki smiled. "But we'll see what you think of me after a little blast of my gun."

"Gun!" someone shouted. "Get his gun!"

Zaki squeezed the trigger of the Positor gun and a ray enveloped the person shouting.

"Oh, forget about the gun," he finally said. "How about a few card tricks?"

Zaki smiled and fired the gun again.

"We must figure out a way to get along," said the Russian representative. "All of this arguing really spoils my lovely day."

Zaki fired the gun once again.

"The Jews are really a very nice people," one of the Arab representatives said. "I think I would like to make a lasting friendship with them."

"Yes, my Arab friends, we have so much to talk and laugh about," the Israeli representative replied. "I have nothing but respect for Mohammed and the Islam religion."

"Judaism is also a very valid religion of the highest sort," one of the Arab representatives said. "I think their concept of God is a very intelligent interpretation of reality."

"Allah is great, no doubt about it," the Israeli shot back. "I think we should read the Koran with great interest."

"The Old Testament is just as good," an Arab shouted. "The relationship between God and Moses was an integral part of human history."

"Yes, Mohammed and Moses would have much to talk about," an Israeli said. "They would have a most interesting conversation with Jesus, too."

"Jesus would like to talk with them very much," the Italian representative interjected. "He would have much to learn and add to a conversation having to do with peace among humankind."

Zaki thought the whole scenario seemed so absurd, yet, seemed to be a much better version of reality than had ever been heard on the planet.

"May we offer you some more land," the Israeli representative said. "We would give anything for real peace."

"No more land," an Arab representative replied. "We already have so much land in the area. Why we have fifteen countries to your one."

"Yes, but we feel a need to give you something to honor our friendship," the Israeli answered back.

"There's no need," an Arab said. "As long as we can make you feel like an honored friend is all we care about. This fighting has gone on too long as it is. It's time we became friends and helped each other."

"Yes, that is our intention," the Israeli responded. "We only want to help you make the region blossom into something great."

"We would have let you help us, but we couldn't accept your religion and your independence."

"But now we also see that we are all brothers in this world and the only thing to do is help one another in an effort to help the planet."

"Yes, I quite agree."

"Yes, and we will help both of you," the American representative said. "We respect the Koran very much and feel it can teach us many things. The Bible and the Koran together is a natural combination."

"Yes, Jesus, Moses and Mohammed will bring great joy to the whole world," the English representative said. "We will share with each other our culture and our beliefs making this a better world for everyone."

Zaki, still smiling, fired the Positor gun again.

"I have always believed that the races should be working together to help everyone," an African representative said. "We will always trust you to work with us to make everyone satisfied."

"Yes, we always believed the African nations and black people throughout the world were our friends and neighbors," the German representative said. "The color of one's skin is such a small difference among all of us and we will consider it like a different color of eyes or hair."

"That is how we always felt," the American representative said. "We are human beings with ethnic differences who have to rely on each other for caring and support and bring equality to everyone."

"We always knew you thought that way," an African representative replied. "We knew that the white world really wanted to be kind to other races and religions, but couldn't because they were embarrassed to make such a fuss about things."

"That is certainly the case," the French representative said. "We have always wanted to make everyone equal, no matter what their religion or color of skin might be."

"That has always been our understanding," the Chinese representative said. "We knew that the world didn't want to cause problems for any of its people."

"Yes, that has always been our attitude," the American representative said. "We always wanted to treat everybody the same no matter where they came from or what they happen to look like. We always wanted to honor any differences and make sure everyone was living in freedom and equality."

"That has always been the way we saw it," the Cuban representative explained. "Everyone has been very willing to accept racial differences and treat everyone as equals in the society."

Zaki couldn't help but laugh. All of human history was now being seen in a positive light. He fired the Positor gun again into the General Assembly.

"We never wanted to oppress anyone," the Russian representative now said. "We wanted a society of equality, regardless of religion and class. We always tried to honor the individual in everything we did."

"No one has ever oppressed anybody," the Chinese representative said. "We have always made attempts to help the less fortunate and make everyone's life a little easier."

"Yes, we have always been shouting about freedom and individuality," the American representative said. "We have always treated everyone with respect and dignity, honoring their right to freedom and the pursuit of happiness."

"Yes, we knew it all along," the Japanese representative said. "You have always been the best country in treating everyone equally and with respect. Black people, Native Americans, Orientals and others have always thought you made them feel very special while living in your society."

"That is very true," the Brazilian representative agreed. "Your society has done much to make everyone feel as if they were free and happy. There was no oppression in your society and everyone was treated equally."

Zaki laughed at the words spilling out into the air. It was something new and different and very refreshing. He watched as many of the representatives grabbed each other's hand and began to sing.

"Michael, row your boat ashore, Hallelujah!"

The singing was harmonious and gentle and Zaki almost wanted to cry. So this was how the world was supposed to be, he said to himself. This was how the people of the world were supposed to behave. He smiled, and then put the Positor gun down and began to walk out of the room.

"Hallelujah!"

Zaki almost had the urge to sing along with them. The world was united as never before, there was no trace of discrimination or oppression anywhere in the room.

"Peace at last," he said to himself, as he headed back to the limousine.

52

It was Cookie's first birthday and everyone gathered at the Friedman mansion to celebrate the momentous occasion.

"Hello, Cookie darling, it's so nice to see you," Sarah Friedman, Zaki's mother, said upon arriving. "You're looking quite healthy."

"I'm working on controlling my id, as Freud called it," she replied, looking up at everyone. "The unconscious is a very powerful force, don't you think?"

"My dear, you don't know the half of it," Mrs. Friedman answered. "Why, sometimes I think I'm walking around using only the unconscious side of my brain."

"Daddy says drinking coffee helps. I can't really say because I'm not allowed to drink it. That is, until I go to college."

"And when will that be?" Marvin Friedman, Zaki's father, asked.

"Very soon," Cookie replied. "Daddy went to college at 11 years old, somewhat old for such education, wouldn't you say?"

"Old?" laughed Mr. Friedman. "Yes, he was quite a geezer."

"Now you don't worry about college right now, little one," Sarah Friedman said. "You just worry about looking cute and learning as much as you can."

"Daddy says we're all monsters," Cookie said with a smile. "He says people may look good, but they're hiding a contentious nature."

"Yes, well, you can't argue with Daddy," Marvin Friedman said. "Where is Daddy, anyway?"

"He's in the laboratory," Cookie answered. "He's trying to bring peace to the world."

"Well, you can't argue with that."

"No, Daddy says when we're finished, everyone will live in harmony. Don't you think that's quite idealistic?"

Marvin Friedman smiled. He was looking down at this one-year-old child thinking she was already as smart as he was. She was definitely Zaki's daughter.

"Yes, I guess so, Cookie dear," he finally said. "But we all have our own dreams about how things should be."

"Very perspicacious, grandfather."

"Don't you have a doll or something, Cookie?" he asked her.

"That is only a form of fantasy, my beloved grandpapa. I am currently exploring the differences between fantasy and reality and have found many interesting elements of each."

"I need a drink," Marvin Friedman gasped.

"Alcohol will only dull your senses, grandfather."

"Yes, definitely a drink. Talk to Jeremiah for a while."

Jeremiah stood there grinning, watching his father be amazed at little Cookie. She was only as tall as their thighs.

"I'll get your drink ready," Mr. Friedman said, walking away.

"Never touch the stuff," Jeremiah replied with a smile. "So where's your Pappy, young one?"

"Did you know that someone who hates everything is called a misomaniac?" Cookie asked.

"Yeah, I've gone out with a few of them," he said. "But at least I found Marna."

"Marna? Who's Marna?"

"That's my girlfriend, little one. She wants to meet you."

"Did you know that *auld lang syne* in Scottish means 'old long ago?'"

"It's August, young one, your birthday, not the beginning of the year."

"Yes, and brontology is the study of thunder."

"You sound just like Zaki did when he was a small lunkhead. Maybe I should have that drink."

"You know drinking urine is part of many non-traditional remedies used today in the world."

"I'm not that thirsty, young one."

Jeremiah was about to walk away when he saw Zaki appear.

"Hello, my genius bro, your little young one is torturing me with everything you used to do."

"She's probably smarter than I was, my young bro. Where are your glasses, Jerry?"

"Oh, I don't need them anymore, Zaki. I have Marna now."

"You threw away the View Finder glasses?"

"I'm in love, not totally nuts, Zaki dear. No, those glasses of yours are probably the best thing you've ever done."

"But you don't need them anymore?"

"No, except when I have nothing to do and want to get in the right mood. You know what I mean?"

Zaki smiled. He looked down and suddenly noticed Cookie standing there.

"We'd better forget about those stupid things—"

"You can forget it, big guy, I heard everything," Cookie said.

"But you won't tell Mommy, will you, darling?"

"For the right price."

"Right price? You're being extorted by your own daughter, Zaki dear," Jeremiah said.

Zaki smiled. "Well, it is her birthday," he finally said.

"What would Cookie like?" Jeremiah asked.

"A big rock," she said.

"Oh, something you can paint on?" Jeremiah replied.

"No, a big rock, ice—"

"A diamond?"

"You got it, young bro," Cookie said.

'Hey, is she really only one?" Jeremiah asked. "I mean she's more conscious than most forty-year-olds."

"I think she is forty at times, Jerry," Zaki said. "Beth and I can't believe how intelligent she is for her age."

"Well, she has the Friedman genes, all right. We spit out geniuses like we own the copyright."

They looked down at Cookie, who was sticking out her tongue.

"Ah, we didn't mean anything by it, little one," Jeremiah told her.

"No offense taken. I'm sticking out my tongue because in Tibet, it's what someone with good manners would do."

"They probably also spit."

"No, spitting is common in Russia to ward off bad luck or to express hope for the future," Cookie explained.

"Well, count me in, little one," Jeremiah said with a smile. "Now I really do need that drink."

"Happy Birthday to you!"

Everybody started to sing as Beth wheeled out a big cake with chocolate icing and a big candle in the middle.

"Happy Birthday, dear Cookie—"

Cookie smiled and stood on top of one of the chairs to see the candle burn.

"Happy Birthday to you!"

"Blow out the candle, dear," Beth said. "But don't forget to make a wish."

"Isn't that a bit superstitious, mother?" little Cookie asked.

"Yes, but that's the custom, darling."

"She's definitely from the Friedman side of the family," Arnold Miller, Beth's father, whispered.

"Oh, we're very smart, too, dear," Beth's mother replied.

"And now for your present, darling," Beth said to her little daughter.

"I hope you like it, my dear," Zaki added.

Everyone looked at the huge box on the lawn, and then when the top was taken off, everyone started to gasp. It was a mini-electric car.

"That's nicer than what we drive," Marvin Friedman complained. "How can they buy a little kid like that a whole car?"

"It's electric, Papa," Zaki explained. "She can't go that fast."

"Any speed at all is fast enough," Sarah Friedman said. "I mean some terrible things can happen."

"I will try to pilot it safely," Cookie suddenly said. "No drinking and driving."

"You let her have alcohol, too?" Mr. Miller asked.

"No, Pa, just a lot of apple juice," Zaki replied. "We prohibit cider."

They watched Cookie get into the little pink car and then slowly drive away.

"Doesn't she need a license or something," Mrs. Miller asked.

"Just be careful, darling," Beth shouted.

Cookie drove down the street and then returned to open her other presents. By the end of the party, she was happy and tired.

'I think I must doze for a moment," she said.

"I know who's daughter that is," Jeremiah said. "Is she going to start snoring now?"

"She's a girl, Jerry," Zaki replied. "She just screams a little."

"Oh, don't I know, Zaki dear."

They all looked at Cookie, who was smiling. "Pneumonoultramicroscopicsilicovolcanoconiosis," she said.

"What the heck did she just say?" Marvin Friedman asked.

"It's the longest word in the English language," she replied.

"Wow," Mrs. Friedman said, "that tops even Zaki."

53

Zaki was encouraged by the Positor gun, but wanted something bigger and more powerful. He decided he would invent the Positor cannon. This would be a huge gun that could fire huge clouds of positive rays. He was determined he would bring peace to the world before he died. He realized the effects of the ray wouldn't last long, but at least there would be peace throughout the world for a few moments.

"This baby can cover large areas," he said to himself with the Thinking Cap strapped to his head. "Maybe I should just shoot it in all directions and see what happens."

The Thinking Cap beeped and buzzed, and then the lights began to flash.

"You need to cut down the distance to register real results," he mumbled to himself.

He began thinking about a craft that would take him all over the world in the speed of light. "The craft will be able to convert itself into a plane, a helicopter, an ocean racer and a submarine," he said out loud.

Zaki unstrapped the Thinking Cap and glanced at the Positor cannon. If it worked, it would be something new in the history of the human race, he said to himself.

"Yes, let's see what this thing is actually capable of," he said with a smile. "The world might never be the same again."

Zaki wheeled the Positor cannon outside the laboratory. He aimed it into the sky and then pulled the trigger.

Thwok!

A huge yellow cloud drifted up into the air. It drifted for a few minutes and then suddenly began to separate and fall upon the landscape below.

"Eureka!" Zaki shouted.

The particles of the huge yellow cloud floated through the air and fell upon a huge area of land and people. Zaki now waited for the results. He walked to a television and turned it on.

"Good evening, ladies and gentlemen, we are happy to report that everyone is getting along well with one another. Some sort of cloud has descended upon a huge area of land and all is well. We have a reporter, Kerry Wilson, standing by. Kerry?"

"Yes, Diana, I'm standing here in Iowa and everyone is smiling. That's right, smiling. The cloud spread across this region about thirty minutes ago, and since that time, there is only silence with no reports of violence of any kind."

Zaki smiled. "The United States is in a state of blissful peace," he said to himself. "Now I'm going to aim the cannon south and east."

He stepped behind the Positor cannon and turned it to the south. Then he pulled the trigger once again. The huge yellow cloud appeared in the sky and then drifted to the south. After a few moments, it descended across Central and South America.

"Peace has come to the New World," Zaki said with a smile. "But I'm not through, yet."

He turned the cannon to the east and began firing again. A huge yellow cloud appeared once again floating to the east.

He then turned the cannon to the north and pulled the trigger. A burst of yellow cloud drifted to the north. He turned the cannon again and again and kept firing in all directions. Clouds of yellow particles drifted in the air over most of the planet.

"That should be enough for the time being," he mumbled to himself. "Now let's see if there's some kind of peace."

He went to the computer and turned it on. "Peace and happiness is reported all over the globe," a headline read on the internet. "Everyone is being very polite to one another and everyone is content."

Zaki laughed. "Yes, finally this planet is going to know what it really feels like to have peace," he said to himself. "Peace on earth."

He was about to go to the television when Beth came running in. "Did you see it, Zaki?" she asked out of breath. "They say peace has come to the world."

"I know," he replied. "I'm the one who did it. Oh, it worked, Beth. The Positor cannon."

"That's incredible, Zaki," Beth said. "You fired it all over the world?"

"There was enough range for the whole planet," he said. "And now everyone will know what it's like to have peace."

"Will it last long?" Beth asked.

"I'm not sure how long it will last, Beth. I don't really know."

"Daddy's invention works very well," Cookie said, upon stepping into the laboratory. "Now all the children will live in peace."

"Hopefully, for a long time, darling," Zaki said.

He moved to the television and turned it on. "There is peace across the planet and no reports of violence of any kind," a male voice was saying. "No one can explain what happened, but everyone agrees it must be the work of a God of some kind."

"A God, Zaki," Beth said with a smile.

"That would be me," he replied with a grin.

"Wait a minute, ladies and gentlemen, there are reports of a rocket being fired in the Middle East. Apparently, the peace that had spread over the planet is over. We estimate that the planet experienced total peace for about 34 minutes and 21 seconds."

"Well, there's your answer, Zaki dear," Beth sighed. "About a half-hour."

"The ray lasted for only 34 minutes?" Zaki said. "Oh, well, it's a start."

"I will help Daddy with the ray when I grow up," Cookie promised. "We will make the ray stronger and it will last for years."

"Yes, hopefully, darling," Zaki muttered. "There needs to be a stronger ray, that's for sure."

"But think about it, Zaki," Beth said. "You brought peace to the world, the entire world."

"But for only a few minutes, my dear."

"Long enough for everyone to get to know what it feels like, Zaki. That's the important thing."

"Yes, Daddy, we will keep trying," Cookie said. "That's the only thing to do."

"The only thing to do, darling," Zaki agreed.

He walked over to one of the chairs and sat down. "Yes, peace," he said. "There was peace for a few minutes."

"That was all you could hope for, Zaki."

"No, I could hope for more, Beth dear."

"Yes, I will help soon, Daddy."

"Yes, my darling, you will help and we will finally do it. We will finally bring peace to the world."

"Well, now you know it's possible, Zaki."

"Yes, possible."

"A possibility is all you need, Daddy."

"Yes, darling, a possibility."

Zaki sat there and thought for a moment. "I'll put on the Thinking Cap," he finally said. "It will help me figure out a solution."

"Maybe all you need is a bigger gun, Daddy."

"Probably, darling. But there was peace for a little while. Peace throughout the world. Anyway, the gyrocraft is almost completed which will be able to take us all over the world in the speed of light. It will be able to convert itself into a plane, a helicopter, an ocean racer and a submarine. Then I'll take along the Positor cannon and there will be finally peace."

Zaki snorted.

"Are you all right, Zaki?"

"I think I must doze for a moment."

"If you think that will help, dear--"

Beth and Cookie glanced at him, but Zaki Friedman was already snoring.